Honeysuckle, Creosote, and Trainsmoke

William O. Cook

MERCURY HOUSE
San Francisco, California

Published in the United States by
Mercury House
San Francisco, California

Distributed to the trade by
Consortium Book Sales & Distribution, Inc.
St. Paul, Minnesota

Mercury House and colophon are registered trademarks
of Mercury House, Incorporated

Manufactured in the United States of America

Library of Congress Cataloging-in-Publication Data

Cook, William O.
    Honeysuckle, Creosote, and Trainsmoke / William O. Cook.
        p. cm.
    ISBN 0–916515–91–5 : $15.95 — ISBN 0–916515–81–8 (pbk.) : $9.95
    I. Title.
PS3553.055474H66   1990
813'.54—dc20
                                                                    90–5841
                                                                    CIP

For Sharon Bratton Hornbuckle and Paula Williams Rice

For Rosemary,
Heres to fond
Childhood memories.
I just Love Memphis!
Peace + Love
William A. Cook
"Bill"
Oct. 11, 1990

Acknowledgments

I wish to express my gratitude to Mercury House, Inc., and the editorial staff for giving me a chance to fulfill a dream.

It is a genuine pleasure to acknowledge John Rollin Williams, Shari Reeves, Kitty Goldstein, Bob Long, Raelene Pell, Steve Aymond, Daniel James, Tracy Gordon, and Steve Wilson for critical readings of the manuscript and helpful suggestions.

I am deeply grateful to Lodie Cook, Jean Brock, L. C. Cook, Charlie McClendon, Elie Lee, Randy Bynum, Billy Poland, and Lester Gonselet for contributions made to this collection of stories.

Special thanks are due to Tuck Kopp, Bess Baskerville, Mary Virginia Kennon, Wayne Reeves, Gary Cathy, Sandy Vinson, Mark Goldstein, David and Roberta Eaves, Sue Anne Carpenter, Alan Haygood, Ken Hornbuckle, Sally Inabnett, Sharon Cook, Danny White, Marshia Davis, Lee Gordon, and Stan Rice for a positive support group of friends.

In memoriam, James E. Smith, James Wiley Cameron, and Cather MacCallum.

Contents

Prologue: Life in the Big House

My mamma and daddy bought the Big House a few months after World War II began. The big old plantation house went for a cheap price because of the war and the increased cost of upkeep. Along with the house came the descendants of former slaves, what was left of them, who had run the massive farm. World War II made things tough all over, and they decided to stay on. My parents didn't have the heart to put them out of the only home they had ever known.

The Negroes lived in the four tiny wisteria-covered, white-washed shotgun houses located behind the Big House. They did all the chores to keep the household running smoothly, just so they'd have a place to belong. Daddy gave them money when they needed it, or when he had some to give. Daddy always said, "The war has made money scarce as hen's teeth."

Big Ruby was by far my favorite, and she was completely in charge of rearing me. She weighed close to two hundred pounds and was as black as river-bottom dirt and just as fertile. I started calling her Big Ruby because of her large size. The name stuck, and everyone called her that. She still wore the starched white uniform of a more prosperous time in the Big House. She was about thirty years old and had four children. The children were all by "different menfolk," as Mamma would say. No one knew for sure who the menfolk were, except Big Ruby, and she wasn't telling. The children were Jake, Jewel, John, and Girthalene.

Jake was a tall, skinny, light-skinned fourteen-year-old, who

1

helped clubfooted Amos with the chores that kept us from starving to death. Muscular Jake looked almost grown. He was very shy, except when it came to the gals. When there were gals around, he would turn into a bundle of nerves, stepping all over himself trying to please. He had clear bluish eyes that gave him a magical look. His blue eyes and light complexion meant Big Ruby had "laid up" with a white man. Sister Jesse was always trying to get Ruby to tell her which white man she let get in her "step-ins." Most people would stop in their tracks whenever Jake gazed upon them with those magical eyes. He had an earthy scent about him, slightly reminiscent of wildflowers and honey, and a little-boyish way that attracted almost everyone, including me.

Jewel was chocolate-skinned, buxom, and very mature for twelve. Like Jake, she also looked almost grown. The young colored men were always hanging around her. Ruby worried about Jewel and was always chasing the boys away, saying, "Jewel, you is like a bitch in heat." Jewel would cry to her mamma, "I's can't help hows I must look and smell to all those ole hound dogs." Jewel had to assure Ruby every day that she was still a virgin, because Ruby did not want her to turn out as she had — a handful of young'uns and no husband.

Jewel's job was to help Jesse and Ruby with the Monday wash. This was done in the big iron pot in the quarters. She also helped iron, cook, can, and care for Girthalene, her baby sister. Girthalene was a typical three-year-old girl child, always under-foot and messing in her drawers.

John and I were the same age, five. He was my very best friend. John was told by Big Ruby to follow me like a shadow, never letting anything harm me. I could not pee without John by my side.

Sister Jesse was what folks called a "redbone." She had bright red hair and a reddish complexion with freckles. Jesse was half–Caddo Indian and half-Negro. She was fifty years old and had never had a man. As a matter of fact, most of the colored people wouldn't have anything to do with her. They called her a squaw.

She took her religion so seriously that Ruby called her a holy roller. They constantly argued about my soul and how Ruby was raising me. Sister Jesse also worked part-time for Miss Neta Palmer, who lived next door to us. Miss Neta was a retired, old-maid piano teacher who was very proper in her mannerisms. Her speech was that of a true southern belle. She took a lot of her time trying to teach Sister Jesse how to speak correctly and other white lady values, so Jesse would fit into the little North Louisiana community.

Big Ruby was very jealous of Miss Neta's attention to Jesse. In turn, Jesse was jealous of the attention my family gave to Big Ruby. In a crisis, though, they stuck together like molasses — just like all colored folks did then. When Sister Jesse would go to nagging and bitching, Ruby would scratch her butt and say, "If that heifer would get some man to give her a good time, she'd stop all that naggin' and bitchin' and be singin' in the cotton all day. Ain't nothin' like a good man to set ya right."

Auntie Mary was the eldest of the three women and the only one who had a recollection of what slavery was like behind the Big House. She still lived in the little cabin where she had been born ninety-six years before. She was a frail little thing with kinky gray hair. Mary was Jesse's great-aunt. Auntie Mary had been ailing in recent years, and Jesse had taken on her share of the chores. Auntie Mary still did sewing for our family and some of the other white ladies in Dixie Roads.

Amos lived in the fourth cabin. He took care of the garden that fed us year round and the yard work. He also cared for the chickens and livestock that put meat on our table. The Big House was self-sufficient except for sugar, flour, meal, and coffee, which we had to get with ration stamps from the store. Amos's notability was his responsibility for most of the beautiful flowered yards in Dixie Roads. Unfortunately, poor Amos was clubfooted. Auntie Mary used to say, "the poor thang don't know whether he's a-comin' or a-goin'." Amos also worked part-time next door for Miss Neta. When he wasn't working in our yard, you could always find him in Miss Neta's flower beds or vegetable garden. He was responsible for Miss Neta's picture-perfect day lilies. Amos was teaching Jake everything he knew about gardening and livestock, so Jake was never far behind him, but John and I were scared to death of the little deformed man.

To my child's mind those people, Big Ruby, Sister Jesse, Auntie Mary, Amos, Jake, Jewel, and John, were more my family than Mamma and Daddy, who were always busy. My character, my imagination, and, most of all, my love for life, were generated from the caregiving of those warm individuals.

Play-Like

The idea came to me on one of those blistering hot North Louisiana afternoons. The bright sunlight came filtering down through the fig leaves, where I was engaged in my favorite game of make-believe—"play-like." The humid, sultry air was laden with the sweet fragrance of honeysuckle and mimosa and had that heavy damp feeling it got just prior to a storm. In late July and August, it seemed to rain around three o'clock every afternoon. It rained just enough to make the air steam and send me running from the fig tree into the Big House, disrupting my visions of make-believe.

The kitchen was always full of people and warm smells. Big Ruby, in her bare feet, was ironing over by the icebox, while Sister Jesse was preparing the evening meal. The aroma of fresh corn, purplehull peas, okra, and fried hot-water bread filled the air.

"Come on in dis house before ya git wet and catch yo' death-o-cold," said Big Ruby. "What ya got on that precious little mind, ya little angel?" She always told me I looked like the angel on top of the Christmas tree, because I had red cheeks and curly blond hair. Ruby showered me with hugs and kisses. In her mind's eye, I could do no wrong. She loved me as much as she loved her own kids.

Jesse chimed in, "Prob'ly thinkin' up some mo' of dem fairy-tale lies you been readin' to him 'bout, Miss Ruby gal. I'm fo'

5

sho' gonna tell the missus when she and Mr. William gits back from the cafe in Ida." Sister was always trying to get my butt whipped. She was a bit envious of the closeness Ruby and I shared.

My parents owned three hamburger-barbeque joints around the Dixie Roads area known as the Pig's Foot 1, 2, and 3. Mr. William and Miss Elsie Matthews, my mamma and daddy, were always at one of the cafes on business. I was left behind with the Negro family.

I sat down at the big kitchen table and said with a sigh, "I want to be the Cotton Queen in a beautiful ball gown and ride down the main street of Dixie Roads in a coach of gold."

Jesse choked on a chicken bone and said, "What a strange chile you is, livin' in all that make-believe world of yourn. Youse try to be jest like yo' sister Gloria Jean."

I sat and listened to them carry on about how Ruby had failed to bring me up in a proper manner.

"This chile is barely five years old and has all dese heah crazy notions you been puttin' in his little head," Jesse sniffed. She crowed and turned a red finger to me, "You mark my word, when yo' parents git home they'll make you cut a switch twice yo' size and tan yo' white booty."

"That's all right, Cotton Candy." Big Ruby always called me by that endearment because of my coloring and sweetness. "I'll play with ya, honey," she cooed. She put down the iron and clicked the radio off. She had been listening to one of those thump-thump-and-bump Negro gospel stations. Turning to me she said, "Come on, let's git out of dis heah hot kitchen and away from Jesse's naggin'."

We went into the parlor. "Let me cool down a minute," she said. She sat down in a Queen Anne chair under the ceiling fan, lifted her dress, and began to fan herself with the fly-swatter. She took a deep breath and said, "I's been thinking 'bout what you said 'bout bein' a queen and all." She hesitated a minute. "You'll be needin' a gown. Let's go up to the attic. I think I know jest the thang."

Hail started beating loudly on the roof as the storm moved in.

The wind must have blown down a pole, for just as we started up the third flight of stairs to the attic, all the electric lights went out.

"I'm affeared we's in fo' a bad storm," Ruby said.

She picked me up and hugged me to her familiar bosom. I loved the smell of her, all warm and safe, smelling of lilac talc and starch. When we got to the top of the stairs, lightning struck close outside, followed by a loud clap of thunder. Shivering, I pressed my face into Ruby's talc-scented bosom. She continued to carry me up the stairs. When she opened the creaky door, hot air, reeking of mothballs, hit us in the face. She put me down and exclaimed, "Whew, Lordy, I can't see a thang. Wait heah a minute." All of a sudden the hot stale air was illuminated. She had found a kerosene lantern. The room was filled with shadows, discarded objects, and the heavy scent of mildew and mothballs. In a low, mysterious voice Ruby said, "Now where could she have put it? . . . There it is." Hanging on a nail was the oddest-looking contraption I had ever seen.

"What in tarnation is that thang?" I asked.

"It's yo' sister's hoop skirts," Ruby replied, clutching her breasts and looking toward heaven. My sister, Gloria Jean, was fond of Ruby, too. Gloria had been gone for over a year. She was fifteen years older than me and had gone off on a train to Washington, D.C., to marry a serviceman. Once I overheard Sister Jesse tell Auntie Mary that I was a mistake that happened when Mamma and Daddy went to Hot Springs, Arkansas, for a hot water cure. I figured that it made them feel so good they got me.

I inquired, "What did she wear that thang for?"

"Oh, it was when yo' sister was Queen of the Cotton Parade over in Shreeport. She was so pretty ridin' on that big float, a sight for sore eyes. There she was sittin' way up high on a throne and all alongside her were her Maids of Cotton — the prettiest white gals in the state. But my Gloria was the prettiest. Jest like sittin' on a cloud . . . Now, let's see if we can find the dress that goes over it." She put the hoops down and bent over a large trunk. Inside were all kinds of clothing articles belonging to my

sister. Ruby reached way down underneath and pulled out a
white dress with a maroon sash, a lacy pair of elbow-length
gloves, and a parasol that matched. I was so excited that I
snatched the dress and parasol and hugged them close. Singing
"Mairzy doats and dozy doats and liddle lamzy divey," a song
Ruby had taught me, I pranced and strutted until I was fairly
dizzy.

"I'll jest take off the bottom hoop and cut the dress down to fit
you. Now let's go downstairs and don't tell nobody 'bout dis. It'll
be our secret." With that, she blew out the lantern.

Parade

The table was set when Mamma and Daddy came in the back door, hot, wet, and tired.

"Hi, ya'll! Watcha do today?" Mamma said, scooping me up.

Ruby took Daddy's wet umbrella, shook it out the back door, and said, "Miss Elsie and Mr. William, ya'll look like half-drowned chickens and as tired as ten mules. I bet ya'll is half-starved to death. Now, ya'll sit down at the table whilst Jesse and me gets yo' supper ready."

I looked up into Mamma's tired gray eyes. She smiled and hugged me close. I then glanced at my daddy. Big Ruby was right. They both looked tired. Mamma said, breaking the silence, "Running a cafe has to be the hardest business a body could get into." She cut a mad look at Daddy and said, "And we have three to run."

My daddy, who never talked much, said, "Well, if we can make it through Christmas, maybe something will change. This war has me so upset. Seems like the end of the world." He and Mamma continued to talk as Jesse put the steaming bowls of food on the table.

While Ruby fed me, I took a good look at my daddy. William Matthews was a small, good-looking man with a head full of coal-black, wavy hair. Most folk thought him too pretty to be a real man, which caused him to get in lots of fights. He wore silver wire eyeglasses, because when he was a boy he had fallen

9

on a stick and put his left eye out. Being half-blind made him very shy. He had never gotten over the fact that because of his poor eyesight the army had rejected him. He hated not being able to defend his country, and he hated being one of the very few thirty-four-year-old men left in the Dixie Roads area.

Mamma had turned thirty-five on her last birthday. She was a bit taller than Daddy, slim and willowy, which was very stylish. She had shiny blonde hair cut in a bob clip. Everyone thought that they were a good-looking couple, especially me and Ruby.

Sister Jesse started to say something but Big Ruby interrupted, "Cotton and I ironed and gathered the eggs."

Mamma cooed and gave me a love pat on the head, "Ain't you the sweetest little thang?"

From outside, the noises of Ruby's children and Auntie Mary came drifting through the back door. They were coming over to get their supper. Jesse handed Auntie Mary's food out the door. The frail, white-haired old darkie turned and gingerly headed toward her tiny front porch. The children got their plates and chose different dry spots in the yard to sit and eat. I'd much rather have been eating out there with John and the other children. Keeping the secret Ruby and I shared was making me antsy.

After supper, Jesse and Ruby cleared the table and began washing dishes. Mamma, Daddy, and I went into the parlor to listen to the big RCA radio. The house was filled with the refrain of "Those Faraway Places." The song was soon interrupted by the announcer with the latest war news. He began, "August 1, 1942 . . ." I became frightened, so I wandered back into the busy kitchen. Sister Jesse cut a piece of watermelon, handed it to me, and asked me to take it down to Auntie because she hadn't been feeling well lately.

" 'Sides," she said, "It's good fo' her kidneys."

I went out the back door and met John at the foot of the steps. "Come on, let's go," I said. "I got something to tell you! Big Ruby and I have this plan . . ."

Auntie was rocking on her front porch and ordered, "Ya'll come on up heah on this porch and set a spell." I loved the look of the little shotgun house with the globelike purple blooms of the climbing wisteria vine dripping off the roof. It shone by the light of the fireflies and the moon. We sat there for a long time, side by side, listening to Mary weave familiar tales in a low, soothing voice. In a few minutes, we were both sound asleep.

As I slept, I dreamt of the beautiful gown and the cart of gold. Through the haze of my dream came Ruby's voice, coaxing us to get up and come to bed. I heard her, but I couldn't move. She picked me up and carried me to my bed. Before she turned out the light, she bent down to my ear and whispered, "When everyone is gone tomorrow, I'll start on yo' gown. Good-night, sugar." My head filled with wonderful dreams.

I was up bright and early the next morning. Once again, the kitchen was filled with lots of sunshine and the smell of bacon frying and hot biscuits. Ruby and Jewel were serving everyone's plates from the stove. Sister Jesse had on her bonnet and was headed for the open market in town. Jake and Amos were working in the flower beds, while John and Girthalene played under the fig tree with Auntie Mary's big yellow tabby cat. The hot air blew tiny yellow butterflies across the yard, brushing lightly against John and Girthalene.

After I finished my breakfast, Ruby told Jake to take John, Girthalene, and me to her house to play. She winked at me as she announced that she had things to do.

Jake led us out of the backyard, down to the dirt road by Auntie Mary's house. There we turned left, proceeding by the old cotton gin. John asked him where we were going. Jake told him we had to go down to the pasture to feed his goat before we could go to the house to play.

To get to the goat's pasture, we had to pass the dreaded Harkness house, a huge run-down barn of a place, with peeling paint and a sinister appearance. The Harknesses had eight children, four of which were boys. Those Harkness boys were four of the meanest boys you could ever want to run into. They always wanted a tariff when we passed, so we cut through the cotton field to avoid being waylaid. We came upon the pen where Bill the goat lived, did our duty, then went to Ruby's to play.

I always loved going to Big Ruby's to play. Ruby and her children lived in the last whitewashed shotgun on the left as you went down the path behind the Big House. A majestic pecan tree rose in their dusty front yard. Attached to the biggest limb was the best tire swing in the civilized world. Jake would take turns swinging us so high, and spinning us so fast, that our legs felt like rubberbands when we landed. Tired of playing and near exhaustion, we went up on the front porch for some cool well water. Jake told John and Girthalene to go inside. He needed to talk to me alone.

We walked along the path to the back of the house where the outhouse was located, and Jake said he had a deal he wanted to work out with me.

"You know that ole tricycle of yourn with the front wheel missing?" he queried as he lowered his overalls to sit down. "What would you take for it? Ya see I's goin' to build this heah goat cart and I needs two more wheels."

A light flashed on in my head. My carriage of gold!

He tore some pages from an old Sears catalogue and stood up. I had never seen a man half-naked before in my life. I couldn't get that sight out of my mind.

"You thinks of what you would take for dem wheels," he reminded me as we retraced our steps to the front of the house.

When we all marched back to the Big House, Ruby sent everyone in different directions. She took me by the hand and led me to the sewing room.

"I finished yo' gown," Ruby announced as she latched the door. "Now youse try it on." She pulled and tugged at the lace, finally turning me around to face a full-length mirror.

Oh, what a sight I saw in that mirror! The dress fit perfectly! She handed me the open parasol as I broke into some fancy footwork. I sang a chorus of "Sweet Georgia Brown." We delightedly placed the dress, parasol, and gloves in a large box and hid them way in the back of one of the closets.

"I's don't know where yo' gonna get your cart of gold, but I's done my part," she said with a broad white smile.

"I'm having one built," I said proudly. She hugged me, calling me a little dreamer.

The next morning I wolfed down my breakfast and headed straight to the garage for the tricycle wheels. I brushed the dirt and spider webs from the wheels, grabbed John from my swing, and headed for Ruby's house to find Jake. He wasn't there, so we figured he had gone down to the goat pen. John and I started walking hand in hand down the dirt road. All of a sudden, four whooping and hollering snotty-nosed boys came out of the tall grass to stand in front of us.

Jimmie Lee Harkness, the eldest, informed me, "You and that little nigger will have to pay a tariff if ya'll plan to go any further."

I told him that we didn't have to pay anything to no poor white trash.

"No? What makes you think you are so high and mighty, you prissy little brat?" Jimmie Lee demanded.

I stuck my nose in the air and replied, "I'm the Cotton Queen and this here is my prince." They all fell on the ground in whoops of laughter.

When they recovered, Jimmie told Buck and John Robert to hold us while the others searched us. All John and I had were a salt-shaker apiece, in case we ran across any green plums or peaches. Jerry Ray grabbed the wheels, tossed them over his head into the weeds, and started to empty our salt-shakers.

I told John to scream as loudly as he could. I screamed bloody murder. They were threatening to beat us up when Jake came bounding out of the cotton patch. The boys scattered, saying that they were going to tell their daddy and we would have hell to pay.

Jake found the wheels in the weeds and handed them back to me. Poor John was so upset that he wanted to go back to the house to lie down.

After we had all arrived safely at the house, Jake and I were left alone on the front porch. Jake said to me, "Well, how's 'bout it, ya gonna give me those ole wheels, Cotton?"

I hesitated a minute and said, "I'll strike a bargain with you, Jake. If you'll promise me I can use that cart every Saturday, I'll let you have them."

Jake thought a minute and said with a little laugh, "Cotton, youse sho' can drive a mighty mean bargain for a five-year-ole chile." But I got my way, as usual.

Once Jake had the four wheels, it didn't take long at all for him to get the goat cart built. The day it was finished, he led Bill into the yard and hooked him to the cart. What fun we all had taking turns getting pulled all over the big yard.

I ran into the house and got Ruby, Jesse, and Auntie Mary. When they saw the cart, Ruby said, "See, Jesse, Cotton's done got his coach. Praise Jesus!"

Jesse retorted with, "Ruby, you an' that chile is goin' to hell in a chinky-pin coffin, a-roarin' and a-poppin'."

I said, imitating Big Ruby, "Oh, hush, Sister Jesse, and just get in." For the first time, I made everyone laugh.

Jesse glared at Ruby and said, "I hates people to shit on my shoes, but I hates even worse fo' um to stand back and laugh at me fo' stinkin'."

Jake rode them all around the yard, one at a time. When we finished, he had to practically carry poor Bill back to his pen. Later, we found some old gold Christmas paint in the garage and covered the whole cart, including the bargained-for wheels.

Now I had to try and talk Big Ruby into making costumes for John and Girthalene. I wanted John to be dressed as a prince and Girthalene as a flower girl. Ruby worked all Friday on the two costumes. She had found some things in the attic that would work just fine. By eleven o'clock that night, Ruby, Auntie Mary, and, yes, even Sister Jesse had finished the costumes. I planned to start the parade the next day, Saturday, at noon. All the shopkeepers would be closing their stores to go home for lunch and a nap.

If you went down the dirt road that fronted our house and turned right, you would end up in downtown Dixie Roads. The little town was built in a wide curve of magnolias. It consisted of a general store, Beason's Grocery, a bank, Doc Parkes's, Miller's Drug, and Pig's Foot 1 Cafe. The main street was still red dirt, with wooden planks for sidewalks.

At lunch that Friday, while our costumes were being made, John, Girthalene, and I went to Beason's for a Grapette and a goober wheel (what we called a peanut patty). We walked up and down Main Street, surveying the parade route, praying it wouldn't rain.

That night, John was allowed to sleep on a pallet beside my bed. We talked, making up stories about how it was going to be tomorrow. We were so excited, it was hard to sleep. The sounds of the night drifted through the open window, and the heavy smell from the hedge of cape jasmine finally put us into a deep sleep.

Ruby awakened us the next morning, fed us, and dressed us in our costumes. John was first. Ruby started by giving him a spit bath. She told John, "Stop wigglin'. A prince can't parade all dirty." She then made him put on four pairs of stockings, with a pair of pink bloomers and a sash at the waist. She added a puff-sleeved blouse with a gold-buttoned vest that had belonged to Gloria Jean. On his head, she placed a folded paper cap with one of Amos's prize pheasant feathers stuck in the side. The outfit was completed by black Sunday school shoes with big silver cardboard buckles taped on top. John was all ready—looking every bit the prince.

Girthalene was next. Ruby put her in a starched pinafore with a veil over her head and face. She carried a bouquet of Auntie Mary's prize tea roses plus a basket of mixed summer flowers.

Then it was my turn. I was given a bubble bath, a hair-washing, and makeup for my face. The final exciting moment came when the dress was lowered over my head and snapped up the back.

We clapped for each other. Then we whisked down the hall to the waiting goat cart. Even Bill had a wreath of flowers around his shaggy neck. Jake put us in the cart and started up the dirt road. Ruby followed behind us at a distance. Jesse and Auntie Mary waved as we wheeled out of sight toward town. We pulled into an alley between Beason's store and the bank. Jake gave John the reins and a small tree switch, telling him to wait until he called to come out.

I asked Girthalene if she remembered the speech we had

taught her. She nodded her little head, "Yeah." You couldn't see her eyes for the veil. We were all nervous as we waited.

Jake finally called, "It's time."

With that cue, Girthalene ran into the middle of Main Street, screaming as loudly as she could, "The Queen's a-comin'! The Queen's a-comin'!" John gave the goat a swat with the switch, and we jerked and bumped onto the busy street.

By now, everyone in town was out of the stores. They turned to see the curious sight coming down the street amid the red dirt and noise.

I was waving. Girthalene was prancing and throwing flowers as the little cart was pulled down the street. Amid the clapping and cheering, we maneuvered our way to the curve and out of sight into the grove of magnolia trees. Big Ruby danced in the dust right behind us.

From that day on, every Saturday of the hot summer, we had our parade. Each time, more and more children joined us in the gaiety.

Payday

Every payday, Dixie Roads was filled with colored and whites alike, doing their banking and shopping for the week. Our parade had been very entertaining to everyone on that first Saturday. John, Girthalene, and I had picked up twenty-two cents in pennies. I remarked to John that we would have to be careful going home because the Harkness boys might bushwhack us and try to take all our money.

After the parade one particular Saturday, we were swooped up by Big Ruby and taken over to the Pig's Foot 1 for a barbequed chicken leg and a Grapette. Because we were with Big Ruby, we had to go into the colored section of the cafe. Ruby thought it was too hot and crowded, so we decided to go outside to eat. We followed her to a shady bench by the filling station.

"Ya'll hurry up and eat now. Dese flies and dis heat are more'n I can stand today!" Ruby exclaimed.

About that time a gangly teenage boy with shaggy red hair and freckles came strutting up. Everyone greeted Buster Miller. His father owned the drugstore.

"Hey, Ruby gal, I've come to take Candy over to my father's store. We're supposed to wait there till Miz Elsie comes in to get her medicine. She said you niggers could go on home and start supper," Buster said. Ruby frowned. She knew my mother would never say "nigger" like that smarty, Buster.

I was clutching my parasol in my right hand, so Buster

grabbed my left and escorted me down the street to his father's store.

We walked into the big cool building. Mr. Miller greeted me with a smile. "My, my, my! Your parades are getting better every Saturday," he said. He took money from some colored children for double-dips on a cone. Then he instructed Buster to watch the store while he ran across the street to the bank for a minute.

When he had gone, Buster led me to the dimly lit back section of the store. He picked me up, hoops and all, and sat me on the ice-cream cooler.

He said, "I was watching you today in the parade. You're the prettiest thing I've ever seen, sittin' up there on that gold coach, waving and blowing kisses to everyone. Ya know I caught one of those kisses myself." I just twirled my parasol. Buster moaned, "Come on, Cotton Candy, don't tease me no more. Give me a real kiss and I'll give you a popsicle." He lunged for me, knocking me off the cooler. We both fell to the floor, with Buster on top of me, all tangled up in my hoop skirts.

Mr. Miller returned just as this occurred and saw us flopping around on the floor behind the cooler. He screamed, "Buster, get off Cotton! What in Gawd's name do you think you are doing?"

Buster untangled his legs from the hoops, leaving me in a heap on the floor. He ran crying to his father, saying, "I didn't mean to do it! I swear, I didn't!"

His father grabbed him and started shaking him, saying, "What! What!" When he finally released the hysterical Buster, he came over to me. He pulled me up off the floor to my feet and said, "What is the meaning of this, Cotton?"

I straightened my dress, picked up my parasol, turned to the crying boy, and said, "Buster, you must be loony from the heat!" With that I prissed out the front door, heading for the safety of the cafe and Mamma.

Buster got the whipping of his life. When Mamma and I came out of the cafe a little later, we could hear Buster screaming from inside the drugstore. Mamma said, "I wonder what's wrong with Buster?"

I didn't see Buster anymore after that day. Ruby said he was sent to military school in Tennessee. She said, "To make a real man out of him." I just twirled my parasol under the watchful, knowing eye of Big Ruby.

Kidnapped

Early one inclement Saturday morning, after breakfast, Sister Jesse told John and me to stop stamping around in her kitchen and to get out into the backyard to play. She was busy making her famous pineapple upside-down cake with pecans for Miss Neta's birthday party that evening. Jesse said, "All the commotion youse a-makin' 's gonna make my cake fall. 'Sides, the way it looks outside there won't be no Cotton Queen paradin' today."

John and I picked up some of my toys and pushed the back screen door open to find the big backyard covered with a wet, thick, smokey fog. The fog was so thick you could barely see the nose on your face.

John turned to me and said, "Ooh-wee, looks like the whole world be on fire and it be smokin'." The spacious backyard that was so familiar to us had been transformed into a hazy, mysterious place with large dark shadows looming up all around us. I took John by the hand as we wandered blindly around, breathing in the damp coolness. Unable to see, we bumped into my swing set. I sat down in the swing, with John standing on the back of it, and began to pump us back and forth through the hazy moisture. We were taking in the new wonders of the transformed yard. Dragging my feet in the dirt, we came to a slow stop.

As the fog swirled, I turned to John and said, "What ya think we ought to get Miss Neta for her birthday party?"

John rubbed his moist nose on his shirt sleeve and said, "I

don't rightly know. She got everthin' a white lady could want fo'."
We sat side by side in the fog, thinking.

I finally broke the silence and said, "Let's go pick her some
wild violets!"

A look of sheer terror passed across John's little round face. He
said in a high-pitched voice, "Cotton, youse got to be loony from
this heah fog. Ya know the only place them violets grows is down
on Low Bayou under the railroad trestle, and Big Ruby would
skin us'n both alive if she caught us anywhere near that train
trestle." John thought for a minute and shivered all over. Gritting
his teeth, he said, "Sss-sides, we would have to pass that spooky
ole Harkness house to get to the trestle and everyone knows the
ole house be haunted!"

I said, "Oh, shuckins, John, ya know those violets be Miss
Neta's favorite flowers. 'Sides, no one can see us in all this thick-
as-pea-soup fog. We'll be down there and back 'fore anybody
misses us." I continued trying to convince John by saying, "Jesse
is busy in the kitchen making her upside-down cake and Big
Ruby is upstairs making up beds and you know she is terrapin
slow when it comes to housecleaning." I changed his mind with
one of Amos's expressions, "Youse jest a pile of wet chicken shit if
you can't go."

John and I disappeared hand in hand through the hole in Miss
Neta's sweet shrub. Carefully wandering around, we finally came
across the little dirt road and headed toward Low Bayou for Miss
Neta's birthday violets.

We walked in the middle of the ruts on the red clay road so we
wouldn't lose our way. The fog swirled up all around. Dark
shadows jumped out at us. The sun peeked out just long enough
for us to catch a glimpse of the big old three-story Harkness
house. It loomed up in front of us, out of the fog, like a giant old
monster. The sight of the half-fallen-down house and the
thought of those dreaded Harkness children sent cold shivers up
our spines. Everyone knew that Bernice Harkness was as crazy as
a Betsy bug. Her mean husband beat her twice a day when he
was home and three times on Sunday. Those nasty, awful chil-

dren had sent the poor woman to the nuthouse over in Pineville twice. An incident involving Mattie, the oldest girl, had sent her to Pineville another time. Mattie had an idiot baby that everyone said was fathered by Mr. Harkness. Mattie left the baby in a sanitarium and ran away to Shreveport. Lula, the second child, had married a fifty-two-year-old man when she was only twelve. They moved to Oil City, leaving the four mean boys and two girls at home.

No one ever saw the two girls. Not so for those nasty, mean boys: Jimmie Lee, Buck, Jerry Ray, and John Robert. They were always getting into trouble. Amos had told us that on moonlit nights, Bernice Harkness would wander on the grounds of the run-down place, wearing nothing but her nightgown, hollering and exposing herself to the full moon.

The ear-splitting sound of the train whistle broke our reverie, sending John and me running blindly down the road. With wildly beating hearts, we found a cow trail that led us through a cotton patch toward the railroad trestle. Climbing underneath it, we searched the sandy, wet ground along the trickling bayou for wild violets. When our eyes finally adjusted to the heavy grayness, we found violets growing among the ferns in great abundance and in all colors. There were clumps of lavender, dark purple, light yellow, and brown. I told John, "Pick as many of the yellow blooms as you can, 'cause they are Miss Neta's favorite color."

In a while, we each had a good-sized bouquet. John said, "We's got enough, Cotton. We better get on back fo' we is missed." We scampered from under the trestle only to find that the fog had gotten thicker. We climbed onto the train tracks. Shoulder to shoulder, we walked down the middle of the crossties in the direction (so we thought) of the Big House. As he clutched the dewy violets in his nervous hands, John said, "Cotton, we has walked and walked till I's almost lame. We must be nearly there by now."

I replied, "Nope, I don't think we are there yet. Jest keep walking."

We finally found a little pig trail and left the tracks. We slid down the rocky embankment and followed the trail until we ran into a wooden wall with peeling paint. We felt all along the high wall until we realized it was the side of a house. John squealed, "Cotton, we made it. We made it back to the Big House!" Excitedly, we followed the peeling wall to the front of the house. Just as we turned the corner, John tripped over a rotted column in the yard. We were pulling ourselves along a veranda rail when the sun came out for a split second, revealing the Harkness house!

Fear shot through us like a cold knife. We both turned to run, when out of the house a low, moaning voice said, "Who is messing around my house?" We froze. Out of the fog onto the veranda came the four hateful Harkness boys. Three of them jumped off the veranda, knocking John and me to the ground. Jimmie Lee, the oldest, yelled to his brothers, "Catch um! Hold um! Ya got um?" as he peered through the fog.

Buck replied, "We got um. Gawd dog, they's as wiggly as wild pigs in a tow sack."

Jimmie Lee said, "Bring um up heah to me."

The three boys dragged us onto the veranda and threw us to our knees in front of big Jimmie Lee. He pulled out his pocket knife as he looked down on us and said, "Well, well, looks what we's got heah. The Cotton Queen and her little ole nigger prince, bringing us some ole bitterweed flowers. I guess we'll jest have to cut their ears off, won't we boys?"

John and I began to cry, when Jimmie Lee reached down and pulled us off the rotted floor by the hair on our heads. I pushed the half-grown bully away as I threatened, "Ya'll had better let us go or I'll tell Sheriff Adcock and he'll lock ya'll up in the ice house and throw away the key."

The snotty-nosed boys slapped each other around and laughed. Then they got into a huddle and began to whisper. John turned his tear-streaked face toward me and said, "Cotton, you has got us into a mess of trouble this time. What's we gonna do now?"

I said in my bravest voice, "Don't ya worry none, John. Someone will find us as soon as the fog goes away."

Jimmie Lee came swaggering over to us and said, "Well, we decided what we's gonna do with ya'll. We's gonna take ya'll upstairs to our hideout and ya'll can consider yoreselves kidnapped! Jest like the Lindbergh baby!" He boasted, "We'll write a ransom note and git us some money for yore hides."

Jerry Ray, between spits, said, "We might get us five dollars for the Cotton Queen heah, but I doubts we gits a nickel for this heah nigger prince." The boys began to snicker as they pushed us through the sagging screen door into the run-down house.

Once inside, looking around, I noticed there was very little furniture. The house was in total ruin. The curtains half-hung on tall, filthy windows. There were cobwebs and dust everywhere. Newspapers and litter covered all the floors. The barn of a place smelled like rot, mildew, and pee. John Robert put his dirty finger up to his tobacco-stained lips and said in a low whisper, "Ya'll had better be quiet, as not to wake up Mamma, or we'll slit yore throats right heah."

The four dirty boys led us up the creaky staircase to the second floor. It was in worse shape than the main floor. Old, sour-smelling mattresses with holes in them could be seen down the dimly lit hall. As we passed, I could see there were no blankets. Jerry Ray said, "This heah is where we all sleep." I held my breath while we proceeded up a smaller, winding staircase to the third-floor crow's-nest room which was their hideout.

In the room, two ratty-haired girls were sitting on the dirty floor playing with soiled ragdolls. Jimmie Lee said, "These heah are our sisters, Vera Ann and Polly June." The filthy girls looked to be about eight and ten years old. Vera Ann, the older of the two, said, "Jimmie Lee, what in tarnation has ya'll done brought us?"

Polly June squealed with delight, "It's the Cotton Queen and her little nigger prince, Sister, and look, they's brought us some flowers." John and I still clutched the violets in our clammy hands. The girls took the violets from us and put them in a snuff jar on the dirt-streaked windowsill.

Jimmie Lee turned to his sisters and said, "Ya'll take care of these heah sissies. Us menfolks has to make us some plans and write a ransom note." He sauntered over to Vera, pulled her to him, and kissed her hard on the lips. As he released her, he said, "Vera, ya watch um and don't let um git away. As soon as we git this ransom money, I'm gonna take you away from this house and yore ole daddy won't be slobberin' on ya no more." The boys ran from the room.

Vera turned to me, straightening her dress, and said, "Yore the real Cotton Queen, ain't ya? My sister and me has seen yore parade, every Sattidy. We never miss one. We shore would like to try on that lovely gown ya wear. Wouldn't we, Sister?"

Polly chimed in, "—and ride in that gold coach and wave at everybody and be somebody."

Vera said, "Well, we is mighty honored ya'll came over to play with us. We usually don't play with no one 'cept our brothers."

Polly said, "Vera, what ya wanna play? We could play mamma and daddy like you and Jimmie Lee do."

Vera said, "Nah. I gits tired of all that huggin' and kissin' and doodlin'."

I breathed a sigh of relief.

Polly said, "Well, we can play like they's our babies."

Vera agreed, saying that she would take the Cotton Queen as her baby and Polly should have the little nigger prince. They picked up the wiggling John and me and sat us in their soiled laps. They rocked us back and forth as they sang to us. John began to squeal and cry.

Polly said to him, "What ya squealin' about, young'un? I bet you has dirtied yore drawers." She pulled John's short pants right off. Then she pulled off his drawers, too. Her eyes got big and she called, "Sister! Sister! Come and look!"

Vera put me down and ran over to see what her sister was acting a fool about.

Polly exclaimed, "Sister, this child is black all over. I ain't never seen nothin' like this." They both just stared at John's naked bottom, shaking their heads, while John cried even harder. Vera finally turned to me. She said, "Now, it's yore turn." The two girls chased me around the little room, eventually backing me into a corner. Just then I heard familiar voices coming from downstairs. It was Big Ruby and Sister Jesse! They were asking Mrs. Harkness if she had seen John and me because we had disappeared in the fog.

Mrs. Harkness said, "No, I haven't seen nobody a-tall. I went to bed with a sick headache and jest woke up now with you knocking."

Vera and Polly grabbed us, muffling our cries with their dirty hands. I bit down really hard on Vera's fingers and started screaming, "Big Ruby! They's kidnapped us! We's up heah! Help! Help! Please, help us!"

The Harkness boys came running into the room with Big Ruby and Sister Jesse right behind them. With one fell swoop and hands slapping, the two big women sent the boys back down the stairs, hollering over the knots on their heads. Ruby and Jesse turned to the girls and asked, "What in Gawd's name is goin' on up heah? What have ya'll done to my babies?" Ruby looked over at John, whose pants were still lying on the floor, and Vera began to stutter. John was crying uncontrollably.

Jesse grabbed the two girls by their matted hair and spanked them all over the room. She threatened, "If I ever catches ya'll around these heah two chilren agin, I'll beat ya to death!"

Ruby put John's pants back on and led us out of the big old musty Harkness house and into the sunny weed-infested front yard. By now the fog had disappeared along with the Harkness boys, less their ransom money but plus sore heads and hurt feelings.

Back in the safety of the Big House, I related the whole story to Big Ruby. After talking the situation over with Jesse, she decided we didn't need any more punishment. We'd had enough from those horrible, sick children. She told us that if she ever caught us anywhere near that house again, she was going to wear us a new bottom!

Miss Neta got some of Mamma's tea roses that night instead of the birthday violets. John and I learned how mean envious people can be. Ruby remarked to Mamma and Jesse, "I think the days of the Cotton Queen are numbered."

The Madame X

During the hot summer months everyone in the Big House observed the hours after lunch as a quiet period. After pushing away from the kitchen table, it was just too hot for us to do much of anything. Often these hours were passed amid warm laughter shared between friends, as we sat underneath squeaky ceiling fans. Occasionally, Miss Neta would bring over some magazines that she had finished and give them to Big Ruby. Ruby's favorite was *True Romance*. Since none of us could read, Ruby read aloud to us.

One day she came across an advertisement for the Madame X Reducing Girdle. The sinful thing was sure to make the fattest lady look like Mae West or your "money back guaranteed!" There were even "before" and "after" pictures to prove the contraption was the greatest thing since mothballs. Ruby got the sewing scissors and clipped the ad from among the naughty pages. Then she pulled the tall kitchen stool, wobbly legs and all, over to the cabinet, climbed up, and reached for the large mason jar labeled "Household Use Only." Among the rationing stamps and spare change, she counted three dollars and ninety-six cents. After removing the money, she returned the jar to its original hiding place.

Sister Jesse, sitting at the table, observed, "If Miss Elsie find out you took that money, she'll skin ya alive, gal!"

Climbing down off the stool, Ruby said, "Ain't no way she'll know nothin' unless you tells her. 'Sides, soon as Miss Neta gives me what she owes me, I'll put it back."

"What she be owin' you fo'?" Sister Jesse asked snappishly.

"She be owing me fo' takin' up the hem in her fancy new Neiman Marcus summer frock." She went on to say, excitedly, how the Madame X would make her the hit of the Saturday sashay!

We met the mailman every day the first week after Ruby had sent for the Madame X, hoping the prize package would be among the other mail. As things go with mail orders, it didn't come until we had nearly given up hope and almost forgotten about it.

One rainy afternoon, the mailman parked his car in the drive and ran up the walk to the front door. He carried a half-soaked box for Ruby. Of course, it was the girdle. The drowsy household suddenly came alive. Once Ruby's shrieks of joy made it through the Big House, everyone met at the kitchen table to watch her open the mysterious brown box, revealing a large sheet of black rubber with pinpoint-sized holes all over it to let in air. Ruby grabbed the rubber thing and held it against her big body, admiring her reflection in the kitchen window.

"Mercy sakes alive! I feel jest like Cinderella!" she squealed. "Come Sattidy, the menfolk's livers will quiver fo' sho' when they sees me in dis heah! Ummm, I'll be so fascinatin' to um, jest like in the *True Romance* stories."

Jesse just shook her head and said, "Ruby, you ought to be 'shamed talkin' that-a-way in front of the chilren."

"Oh, shoots," sighed Ruby. "these chickens don't know what ole Ruby's a-sayin', do ya?"

We all shook our heads no. All we knew was that her excitement was contagious.

The long-awaited girdle had arrived on Thursday, and we all felt that Saturday would never come. We couldn't wait for the transformation to take place, just like in the before-and-after pictures in the magazine.

Friday, the coal-oil lamps burned half the night down at Auntie Mary's shotgun house. Everyone was helping Big Ruby ready herself for the stroll through the streets of Dixie Roads. After hearing of Ruby's plans to make herself more beautiful, Miss Neta had brought over to Auntie Mary's a dress with dots the size of silver dollars. She also gave Big Ruby some of her beauty tips, which Ruby said she must have stolen from a horse doctor. Ruby didn't think too much of Miss Neta's beauty secrets, especially after the time Miss Neta put Glovers Mange Cure on her scalp to rid herself of dandruff. Miss Neta lost nearly every hair on her head.

Auntie was over in the corner under a strong lamp taking up the black and white polka-dot dress by hand. Her bigger-than-life shadow blackened the newspaper-covered wall behind her. With a hot curling iron in her hand, Sister Jesse had plopped Ruby down in a chair by the wood stove. Now she was busy burning Ruby's kinky hair into the latest forties hairstyle, which she was trying to copy from the Sears catalogue.

Trying to keep Ruby from wiggling, Jesse said, "Girl, dis hair is so nappy! Now, hold still 'fore I burn ya, you heah!" As she applied more Royal Pomade Jelly, she said, "Mmm, I don't know how you 'spect us to make a silk purse out a ole sow's ear."

John and I were watching the whole commotion from our positions on the oiled floors. Smelling the familiar odor of burning hair, I turned to John and asked, "Won't that make her hair fall out?"

He replied, "Nah, all colored folks press dey hair dat way. Don't you know nothin', Cotton?"

I don't think any of us slept a wink that night. I know, for sure, that Ruby didn't. In order not to mess up her new hair-do, she had propped herself up in a straight-back chair all night.

The sashay through the streets of the little cotton town started early on Saturday morning. Dressed in their Sunday-best clothes all the field hands and country colored people would come into town that day to do their week's shopping. They would stroll up and down the red clay streets from one end of town to the other, sporting their bright clothes, spit-shined shoes, and heavily pomaded hairstyles. It was a fact that Saturday mornings belonged to them, and no white person in his right mind would go into town during that time.

Shortly after breakfast, the final preparations were under way. In the middle of the house was Auntie Mary's big feather bed, covered in quilts, with Big Ruby stretched across it.

Jesse said, "Jewel, you and Auntie come over and set on this cow's back so I can fasten dis thang up." Jesse pulled and tugged to no avail. Out of breath, she panted, "Come on, John, you and Cotton climb up heah and git on and hold on tight, now." Finally, after a lot of grunts and groans, Jesse got all the strings laced up. The horrible contraption covered Ruby from her fat neck to her flabby thighs. When we climbed off, we couldn't hear her breathing anymore.

"Jesse, Mamma ain't breathin' no mo'!" cried Jewel.

John looked at me with big black eyes and said, "Cotton, I think my mammy's dead."

Jesse yelled, "Ya'll help me turn her over. Now, one-two-three, push!" With a shove, we managed to turn her onto her back. Suddenly, there was a terrible hiss and gasp of air just like when a Coca-Cola bottle is uncapped!

"She's alive!" I screamed. "She's alive!"

We pushed Ruby off the bed and onto her feet. She teetered, grabbed the bedpost, and stood on her shaky legs. Her eyes were bulging out of their sockets.

"Look, ya'll! She's thin as a rail!" exclaimed Jewel.

Jesse said, "I sho' don't know where all that blubber done gone to."

I figured, by the way she looked, that it must have all gone to her neck, arms, and legs.

Very carefully, Auntie Mary slipped the polka-dot dress over Ruby's marcelled hair-do. Next came the tomato-red lipstick Mamma had given her for the event, dashes of vanilla extract from the kitchen for the hem of her dress and behind her ears, and baking soda for under her arms.

Jesse reached down and put some vanilla behind Ruby's swollen knees and said, "Jest in case she does pick up a man! Amen, thank you Jesus!"

"Mamma, you be as perdy as a speckled pup. 'Sides, I always wanted a daddy," remarked Jewel.

Returning from the closet, Auntie Mary had a shoe box with her. "It's time fo' Cinderella to put on her new shoes," she said. She opened the box, took out the tissue paper, and exposed a brand new pair of tiny black patent-leather heels. The new shoes had belonged to Gloria Jean. She had never worn them and my mamma had stuck them back in the attic.

Jewel looked at the shiny little shoes and then at Ruby's big feet and said, "Be like puttin' a camel through the eye of a needle to put those in there. Heah, Mamma, sit down on the side of the bed."

"I can't sit down, chile," Ruby said. "You'll have to put um on whilst I'm a-standin'." The whole time, her voice sounded like air being let out of an inner tube.

Ruby lifted one leg and clutched the bedpost tighter. John and Jewel struggled to get her oversized, flat feet into the small pair of black heels. Jewel said, "Double yo' toes under. Push! Push hard!"

Auntie Mary suggested some vaseline as a remedy. "Heah, try this," she said in her shrill voice. "You can put some o' this on a hoe handle and shove it up a gnat's ass!"

With a little vaseline applied to the heels, Ruby's big calloused feet finally slipped into the little shoes. Her swollen ankles spilled over the sides.

Shoes in place, we grabbed Big Ruby and very slowly walked her through the screen door onto the porch. Auntie Mary hooked a black purse around the crook of her elbow and said, "Honey chile, you looks so perdy! Jest like in the picture books! Is you all right, sugarplum?"

Ruby took a big gulp of hot air and pooched out her cheeks. She crossed her swollen eyes and nodded yes.

We helped her off the porch, across the yard, and onto the dirt road that led to town. Once on the road, we all let go of her. She took three steps backward, then jolted forward in a half-run, half-walk stride. She walked on the sides of the little shoes and made her way down the hot, dusty road toward town, zigzagging from one side of the road to the other. When she was out of sight, we took our places on the porch and weaved tales about what Ruby was doing in town.

About thirty minutes later, we heard the most awful hollering from down the road. We ran from the porch and saw Big Ruby stumbling back. She was screaming like a madwoman, "Git me out of this gawd-damn thang! Please, git it off!" all the while pulling at her sweat-soaked dress.

We ran to her as she collapsed in the red dirt. We dragged her wet body to the shade of Mary's porch. By then, she was in a dead faint. Auntie Mary ran inside, got a dipper of water, and threw it in Ruby's makeup-smeared face. She had also grabbed a pair of scissors, which were to prove helpful to us.

"Ya'll turn this heifer over now, don't jest stand there gawkin'!" she ordered.

Together, we managed to get her onto her stomach. Jesse reached down and ripped open the buttons of the polka-dot dress. Mary cut the knotted laces of the torturous Madame X. When the last lace had popped, Ruby's large black body poured out all over the small porch like a bale of wet cotton. Where the pinholes had let in air, there were clear little blisters, which in a week's time would make Big Ruby peel like a snake.

The revived Ruby said she had learned her lesson about trying to be something she wasn't. From then on, she would just have to be satisfied being fat. "'Sides, all the colored men like big-assed, big-tittied women! And dat's a fact!" she said with a wink.

Auntie Mary's Bag

Mamma and I were sitting in the kitchen having iced tea when Auntie Mary appeared at the back door with her dead cat cradled in her arms. Auntie explained to us that she had awakened that morning to find her beloved cat, a yellow-and-white tabby, at the back door, dead. Since she had been ailing, just watching that cat prance and play around the yard had given her much comfort.

Auntie Mary said, "Rat pizen from the cotton gin must have killed my cat!"

Mamma told her not to bury it in the yard because the dogs would dig it up and spread it all over creation. Dismayed, Auntie took the corpse back home. Of course, my curiosity got the better of me, so I followed her to see what she would do with the dead cat.

Auntie was supposed to take the noon bus to Shreveport for a doctor's appointment that day. She said to me, "I'll jest put it in a sack and shorely I'll find somewhere along the way to git rid of it."

She wrapped the cat in waxed paper and then stuffed it into a Neiman Marcus bag that Miss Neta Palmer had given her to save. Miss Neta did all her shopping in Dallas, Texas. That is where she got the bag. Since the war had begun, Mary saved everything — paper sacks, strings, rags, jars — anything she could think of a use for.

With the Neiman Marcus bag firmly in her gloved hand, Auntie Mary put on her straw hat and set out for town to catch the Shreveport-bound bus. I was left behind to wonder what she would do with the cat.

She stood in the hot sun in front of Beason's store for about half an hour waiting for the ever-late bus. With a stop every half-mile to pick up shoppers bound for the city, the trip took over an hour. When Auntie finally arrived, she was exhausted and covered with perspiration. Faint and half-starved from the long trip, she grabbed her package and headed for the Colored Only section of the bus station.

She virtually dove into a glass of iced tea and relished her cool chicken salad sandwich. They both provided her with much needed relief. After eating, she became very relaxed, pulled one foot out of its shoe, and began to snooze. She slept until the waitress brought her back to life by saying, "This ain't no hotel, honey. Youse better mosey on."

Jerking awake, Mary realized she was late for her appointment with the doctor. Instantly she jumped up, put her foot back into the worn shoe, and hobbled out onto the blistering street.

After her appointment was over, she reached down to pick up the bag that held her cat, but it wasn't there. She searched the office to no avail. Back out on the street, she frantically headed in the direction from which she had come, ending up at the bus station. She entered the colored section once again, looking high and low for the bag. It was not to be found. She walked outside, scratching her head, and glanced through the sun-streaked window one last time. There it was, sitting at the feet of an old colored woman! The woman was eating quickly and glancing from side to side very anxiously. She checked constantly to see if the bag was still there. She couldn't wait to get home and discover what her stolen Neiman Marcus prize was!

Auntie, of course, couldn't wait to get home either, so she could tell us the story of how easily she'd disposed of the dead cat.

Honeysuckle, Creosote, and Trainsmoke

During the forties, everyone's life was touched in some way by the railroad. The tracks lay about a hundred feet behind Big Ruby's shotgun and continued behind the cotton gin, snaking out through the cotton patches all the way to Texarkana and beyond. My parents would set their watches by the passing trains, as did half of Dixie Roads. Cotton farmers depended on the railroad to take their bales of newly ginned cotton to market. The business folks depended on the black locomotives to bring needed supplies into the small town. Everyone used the railroad for transportation. The sad thing about the trains was that they took all the young men from Dixie Roads to fight the war, leaving Daddy behind. It seemed that five or six times a day, and into the night, the big rumbling trains would interrupt our thoughts and set everyone to thinking of "Those Faraway Places" — the song we heard so often on the radio.

From Big Ruby's front porch, you could get a good look at the lightning-fast trains as they whizzed by. John and I made up games pertaining to the passing trains. We would make bets on how many boxcars would be on the long trains. Sometimes there were way over a hundred, with two engines and two cabooses. We both always got a sinking feeling whenever the caboose went by, like we had lost something. The train conductors and passengers would wave to us, and if the engineer saw us in time, he would blow the eardrum-splitting whistle.

If the wind blew in the right direction, the thick black smoke would come billowing up on the porch to engulf us in a mysterious fog, putting out the sun for a few seconds. Oh, how we loved the smell of the heavy trainsmoke mixed with the sweet smell of the honeysuckle, which grew in abundance over the creosote-soaked crossties!

The pungent mixture of creosote and the fresh perfume of the honeysuckle would trigger fantasies in our minds about Washington, D.C., St. Louis, and New York City, all those places we never expected to see — except in our dreams. The passing of the colorful boxcars had a very special meaning for John and me. What we had once seen in a boxcar was one of our biggest secrets.

The brightly painted cars had been sitting idle on some side tracks for about two weeks right beside Big Ruby's house. I remarked to John, "I wonder how come those boxcars are sittin' over there empty. I guess they'll get cobwebs on um 'fore they move um."

John replied, "Let's us go see what's wrong with um." We made sure that no one was looking and ran across the ditch, where the redbugs lived in the weeds, to see if we could figure out why the boxcars hadn't been moved. As we were checking out the cars, we heard voices coming from inside one of the boxcars. We started to run away when I recognized Jake's voice. I said to John, "Wait a minute, that's Jake talking in there."

John said, "Yeah, but who is that gal I heah in there with him?"

We tiptoed very quietly through the honeysuckle vines growing in the gravel over the rarely used side tracks. Following the sound of the voices, we ended up in front of a half-opened Kansas City Southern boxcar door. We peeked in through the dusty light. Jake was squirming on top of someone, naked with his butt high in the air. We could see long white legs under his slick brown body.

I whispered to John, "Who is that gal under Jake and what's he a-doin' to her?"

John's eyes were so big, they were almost standing out of his head on a stem. He said in an excited, hushed voice, "Cotton, you shouldn't be lookin' at this heah."

Jake must have heard us, because he got off the girl and hollered, "Who's that out there?"

John and I scampered under the car next to the big rusty train wheel. From our hiding place, we could hear Jake walk over to the door. We heard him say, "Who's out heah spyin' on me?" We huddled closer together. Jake stood a while longer before saying to the girl, "I guess it was the wind out there. I didn't see nobody. Now, sugar, let's us get back to what we was a-doin'."

When we heard the gal squeal, we came out from our hiding place and continued to watch the strange sight in the dusty light. By now, we could see that the girl was Vera Ann Harkness.

We left the two of them in the boxcar and ran back to Big Ruby's porch. John and I began to giggle excitedly over the secret wrestling match we had witnessed. From then on we would tell it to each other with breathless excitement, over and over, whenever we were alone.

Later that same afternoon, John, Girthalene, and I were playing with a piss ant under the house at Ruby's when we heard in the distance the rumbling of the two-thirty coming from Shreveport. From the sound of it, it was coming lickety-split. The noise made all of us very excited.

"Oh, let's us go closer and get a better look," I said.

"Cotton, you know we ain't s'pose to go no further than this heah," John answered hesitantly, "or we'll get the tar beat out'n us by Big Ruby."

Looking around the yard, I said, "Oh, shoot, John, there ain't nobody around to see us, they's all up at the Big House. I double-dog-dare ya, you big titty baby."

John couldn't stand a dare. We grabbed Girthalene out of the dirt and ran across the little sweet potato field. By then we could see the huge monster coming toward us, huffing and puffing and hissing steam. We jumped under a trestle bridge just as it passed overhead. The hot-sparked air blew all around us, engulfing our whole bodies in fiery excitement. Afraid to look up, we all three crouched in a little huddle and, facing each other, began to scream at the tops of our lungs. We screamed until the noise from the great, rumbling train overhead had deafened us and we could no longer hear our screams.

John looked up, pointing to the caboose. We lay back in the dirt and waited until we could hear again. Then John said with wide eyes, "Did ya'll see what I saw?"

Girthalene and I shook our heads no. "You mean to tell me ya'll didn't see that ole hobo jump off the train?" John asked in disbelief.

"If there was a hobo, where did he go to?" I asked.

John replied excitedly, "He jumped off the train, and he rolled over and over, and then he done got up and disappeared over yonder!" He pointed along Low Bayou to a little willow thicket. "He sho' was a mean lookin' un. I jest wonder if he might be a 'scaped convict," he added with a shudder.

"What did he look like?" I asked.

John's already wide eyes got even bigger as he told us, "He got him a long beard and a tow sack over his shoulder and he be dirty as a hog."

I said, "He's prob'ly bein' hunted down this very minute by the FBI—"

"—Or maybe the high sheriff!" John said.

With that, Girthalene began to cry. I quickly went over to her and tried to comfort her by saying, "Nah, he's jest a poor ole hobo who is trying to hitch a free ride to D.C. and got off here to steal some chickens or something."

As she stopped crying, John reached out and took Girthalene's little hand. He said, "We better git back and tell Amos and Jake to lock up all dem chicken coops. One day they caught a hobo in the chicken house at midnight, eatin' a raw chicken, feathers and all. 'Sides, he might try and take us off in dat dere tow sack."

That made poor Girthalene holler again, louder this time, as she clung to John.

By now, I was really curious about who was over in that thicket. "Come on," I told them, "let's see if we can pick up his trail and see what he's a-doin'."

The very idea made John stop and shake in his tracks. Girthalene stopped crying out of sheer surprise.

"Cotton, youse got to be crazy as a loon," declared John.

Pulling my pocket knife out of my overalls, I opened it and said, "If he gets us in that sack, I'll cut us free and then I'll cut his gizzard out and feed it to the dogs."

I jumped around stabbing the air, convincing the two of them that I would protect them to the death. We would just follow him to see what he was doing. If he was up to no good, then we could run and get Sheriff Adcock and have him locked in the ice house. With that, we started out on the hobo's trail.

We followed a cow path down to Low Bayou. The path ran under a trestle and ended in a honeysuckle thicket. "Sshh!" I warned. "Be real quiet. Do ya'll hear anythin'?"

"Not a peep," replied John.

Listening for a moment, I said, "Let's see if we can smell him out."

We put our noses in the air like Amos had taught us to do when tracking a coon. All we smelled was the sweet honeysuckle surrounding us. We got down on our hands and knees and crawled over to a little clump of willows. As we looked into a clearing next to the banks of the bayou, we finally saw him. He was bent over a small fire and seemed to be cooking something in a large can.

John punched me in the arm and asked in a low whisper, "What's he a-doin', Cotton?"

"It looks like he's cookin' a rabbit," I replied, pointing to a bloody skin that was pinned to a willow trunk with a hunting knife. The smell of woodsmoke and cooked meat floated over to where we were hiding in the damp willows. The hobo reached into his tow sack and produced a huge sweet potato. He sliced it with his pocket knife and dropped the orange chunks in the simmering can. Then he stood from his squatting position and began to search along the little bayou. Every so often, he would stop, pick a few leaves, and pull up a root or two.

After he washed the leaves and roots in the bayou water, he returned to the can and dropped his findings into the boiling liquid. When he finished that chore, he pushed some damp leaves into a pile. He laid his coat over the pile and stretched his long body out on the leaf bed. Not long after he crossed his legs, he was snoring.

I turned to John, "I double-dog-dare you to run around the fire and look to see what's in that there can and run back over here without waking him up."

"After you, you coward!" snorted John.

"No, you are the coward!"

It was decided we both would go on the count of three, leaving Girthalene in the thicket where she was content, playing with a doodle bug in the sand. John and I tore out of the thicket like wild Indians, rounded the fire, spit in the can, and headed back to our leafy hideout.

"What the — what in the hell is all the racket!" gasped the big man as he jumped to his feet and ran to the willow for his hunting knife. As the hobo headed for our thicket, we jumped down into the wet reeds. We grabbed Girthalene, knocking her thumb out of her mouth, and squeezed her for dear life as we closed our eyes tightly. With her thumb out, Girthalene began to scream. The mean-looking man bent forward and pushed aside the willow branches.

"What in the world do we have here hiding in the willows?" he asked.

We must have been a strange sight — John and I squeezing the daylights out of poor squalling Girthalene!

"Come on out of there, I'm not gonna hurt ya. I just want to talk to ya," he told us in a low voice.

We got to our feet. Slowly we came into the clearing, pushing Girthalene in front.

"What are you and these little pickaninnies doing out here alone?" he asked me as he led us to the open fire and told us to sit down.

"We are running from the law, jest like you are," I told him.

He scratched his bearded face. "What makes ya'll think I'm runnin' from the law?"

John said, "It jest makes sense, you jumpin' off trains and hidin' in the woods like this heah."

The young man laughed, "That a fact? Well, I'll tell ya what, if you start telling me the truth, I'll tell you the truth. Deal?"

"Deal!" we exclaimed in unison.

"You go first," I said.

"No, you go first."

"Well, Mister, what do you want to know?"

"Where do ya'll live—and what were ya'll followin' me for?"

I began, "Well, sir, we all live across the railroad tracks in the Big House and we saw you jump off the train and run into the thicket. We followed you to see what you were gonna do. That's all we were doing."

He said, "Ya'll are powerful brave to follow the likes of me. Does anybody know where ya'll are at?"

We shook our heads no.

He pulled a tobacco pouch out of his top pocket and rolled a Bull Durham cigarette. He said, "Well, if ya'll are so all-fired curious 'bout me, then I'll jest have to tell ya."

He handed me a big spoon and told us to help ourselves to the mulligan stew. "Ya'll gonna have to use the same spoon, as I wasn't expectin' company," he laughed.

He leaned back on his elbows. Taking a long drag on the hand-rolled cigarette, he said, "Now, when the big war broke out, I had a new wife and I had a new business—jest taken over my family's grocery store. I was sittin' pretty. Then that ole war came along and ruined everything for us. I got so much pressure from my wife and the town folks about joining the service, it like to drove me crazy . . ." He took another drag and went on. "Everybody said I should go and fight for my country to keep it free. They said I was twenty-two years old and the war needed strong young men to fight. Well, I'll tell you, I never killed a thing in my life except to eat, and I jest couldn't see myself killing a man. I started to have nightmares and couldn't sleep at night. One day I got my orders in the mail to report for my physical. I jest tore it up and closed the store. Jest locked 'er up and walked out of town with a little money and the clothes on my back and hopped a train to nowhere. I been all over this here United States about twice, always avoiding the law." With tears in his blue eyes, he looked at us and asked, "Did ya'll know it is against the law not to fight for your country?"

He looked very sad as he told his tales about all the places he had seen and the things he had to do just to stay alive. One minute he would be laughing and the next he would get all choked up.

Suddenly, out of the haze of the hobo's stories, we heard our names being called. "Cotton! John! Girthalene! Where are you?"

The young man once again jumped to his feet. He grabbed his meager belongings and was gone like a shot, leaving the three of us sitting by the fire, mesmerized.

Into the clearing came Big Ruby, Mamma, and Sheriff Adcock.

Ruby said, "There they is! Git up! Look at ya'll! Where did ya'll git the matches to build this heah fire? I's got a good mind to switch ya'll when we gits you home. I's told ya and told ya not to play with fire. It makes ya pee in the bed."

Mamma said, "Ruby, hush all that chatter. Thank God, they are all right!"

Sheriff Adcock kicked the little fire out with his boots and said, "Miss Elsie, you need to beat their little asses. Uh, pardon me for cussing, ma'am."

Mamma said to him, "That will be all. Thank you so much for your help, Sheriff, but we don't beat asses in my home. However, you can rest assured these children will be punished."

Mamma and Ruby grabbed our hands and led us out of the thicket. As we walked beside the tracks, we heard a train coming around the curve. We stood back as the loud engine roared past, spitting out shiny sparks. We looked just in time to see the young hobo come bounding out of the woods and hop onto the fast-moving train. He crawled up the side of the boxcar to the top, stood there for a minute, and waved. Then he disappeared between the cars as the train pulled around Dead Man's Curve and out of sight.

"Did ya'll see that?" Ruby asked. "An ole hobo a-wavin' at us!"

John and I sneaked a look at each other and smiled really big.

"Cotton, John, who was that man?" Mamma inquired of us.

We knew we were in trouble, but we never told them about our new friend. In our secret moments, John and I would talk about him and think about Vera Ann and Jake and the sweet smell of honeysuckle, creosote, and trainsmoke. Out of the trainsmoke, we would see the young hobo's sad face and hear his lonely tales.

Amos

On a cold December morning, in a cypress-log shotgun, long before my parents bought the Big House, the colored woman Hattie Lee gave birth to a small, deformed baby. She named him Amos. His poor little clubbed feet were put on backward by God.

By Christmas, Hattie Lee had run off with a cotton picker by the name of John Lucas, leaving behind little Amos — buck naked and squalling in his crib. Auntie Mary, Sister Jesse, and Ruby, who was only a small child herself, took on the responsibility of raising the deformed baby. At that time, Sister Jesse's brother, Jacob, did all the chores that Amos would learn and take over after Jacob's death.

Jacob's and Jesse's father was an African slave, not a common slave, but a witch doctor. He was so vital to the running of the massive plantation, he was treated like royalty by the owners. In a lavish celebration, the witch doctor married a Caddo Indian maiden, Little Duck. (That is where Sister Jesse got her Indian blood.)

The witch doctor passed down all his knowledge and secrets to Jacob, who in turn passed them to Amos. Amos knew more about planting and harvesting vegetables, cultivating flowers, raising and slaughtering animals, hunting, fishing, tanning hides, and folk medicine than anyone else in Dixie Roads. As a matter of fact, he knew more than anyone in the parish. Whites and Negroes alike came from miles around, stopping by the spotless shotgun to chat and try to get "sly Amos" to reveal some of his secrets. He lived in the very same house where he was born.

One bone-chilling day in November, Auntie Mary came down with pneumonia. Doc Parkes was summoned but shortly gave up on the sick old woman. The doctor remarked as he was leaving, "I've done all I can do. I'll have to leave her in the hands of the Lord."

When he was gone, Amos brewed some chicken-shit tea with mullein and a drop of whiskey. He made Auntie drink three cups a day. The fever broke on the third day, and Auntie Mary was on her way to recovery.

Doc Parkes never spoke to Amos again. Mother overheard him say down at the cafe, "That little nigger has made me the laughingstock of this here town with his chicken-shit tea!"

"Horseshit," Mamma said.

"No, chicken shit," replied the doctor.

Mamma said later, "This town, huh! He should have said this whole damn parish. Amos knows more about medicine than that educated doctor. He saved Auntie, didn't he? Who would have ever thought of drinking chicken shit? Oh! Murder!" she gagged.

Amos made pads out of leather to strap to both his knees, so he could work in the low flower beds. He would pull himself from bed to bed and all around the yard on big, strong arms and calloused, oversized knuckles. He worked better using his strong arms as feet instead of the clubs he was born with.

Jesse said, "Amos can do more work in a little while than most field hands can do in a day."

Ruby would look out the back screen door and remark, "Would ya look at dat little colored man work! Jest like a monkey down there so low to the ground."

Hearing Big Ruby, Amos would do cartwheels and walk on his hands, smoking his pipe. She would stand at the screen and scratch her rag-tied head as she died laughing.

Then Ruby said, "It's curious to me how all dese heah so-called healthy folks can ask Amos to do all their work while they go set in the shade in an easy chair on their asses and watch. Unh, unh, unh! I guess they gits some kind of weird pleasure out'n it. But who'm I to say? Only the good Lord knows fo' sho'. She would sing sweetly the hymn, "Swing low, sweet chariot, comin' fo' to carry me home . . ."

John and I were scared to death of Amos. He was truly a strange-looking sight, so mysterious and quiet when he moved around on his hands. He was always sneaking up on us when we were playing. He scared the pee right out of us.

Ruby would put down the ironing and stand at the back door hollering, "Amos! You stop scarin' them young'uns, ya little piss ant. I don't want to have to change their drawers." They laughed and we cried.

Amos would pull himself up into a mulberry tree in the side yard and hide in the thick green foliage. He ate the tasty berries and smeared the crimson juice all over his face and coveralls. When he had had his fill, he would swing down to the ground, looking like a bad little boy, and scare us again. The juice from the sweet berries looked just like blood.

Amos was totally responsible for Miss Neta's lovely flower gardens, and every year — because of him — she ran away with almost all the blue ribbons at the Day Lily Show in Shreveport and the Camellia Show in Texarkana, Arkansas. But to hear Miss Neta tell it, it was quite a different story. She would say, "I get up every morning at the crack of dawn and work my poor fingers to the bone, a-weeding and a-pulling. That's why I win all these blue ribbons for my lovely flowers."

Ruby would say, "All Miss Neta do is take credit fo' all the hard work Amos do over in those beds. All she do is go out and pick a few and get all in poor Amos's way with 'do dis heah' and 'do dat dere.'"

One of those quick thundershowers that are so familiar to Louisiana came out of nowhere one morning. The rain came down in buckets with the sun still shining — a real frog-strangler. John, Girthalene, and I were caught under the fig tree with Amos. As the rain came pouring down, we huddled in a wet bunch under the branches of the tree. Amos began to jump up

and down and speak in an unknown tongue. He threw his
muddy little body all over the ground in a wild frenzy. The rain
stopped as abruptly as it had started, and so did Amos. We wiped
the rainwater from our eyes to see Amos sitting in a mud puddle
staring up into the sky. The bright sun had made a rainbow.

None of us had ever seen such a sight. Amos told us that with
all his commotion he had made the rainbow. He said, "Ya'll know
there be a pot of gold at each end." He pointed across the house
to one end and clear across behind the cotton gin to the other
end, then scooted across the yard, lickety-split, saying he was
going to get that pot of gold. In hot pursuit, John and I followed
the little man to the end of the yard. Unable to keep up, we
stopped in time to see Amos disappear behind Miss Neta's sweet
shrubs. He didn't appear again until long after supper — without
the gold. When we asked about the gold, he chuckled and said,
"It faded away 'fore I could git to the end. But by Gawd, next
time I sees a rainbow, I's gonna git dat pot o' gold." We all went to
bed that night thinking about gold, and how if Amos hadn't been
so slow we would have been rich.

One day, after the rainbow, John and I slipped down to Amos's
to find him not at home. I said to John, "Where do you think he's
a-gone to?"

John scratched his little burr head and said, "He prob'ly gone
a-fishin', or maybe he went to kill a rabbit for supper."

I looked around outside. John came up behind me, grabbing
me with both hands around my neck, and said in a mean voice,
"I caught ya boy, snoopin' round my house."

I pushed him away with, "You like to have scared the daylights
outta me. I thought for shore you was Amos."

Looking the place over, we discovered that Amos had a garden
planted with fresh herbs and flowering medicine plants. In
between the rows of mustard greens, tomatoes, snap beans, okra,
and collards, he had planted rows of marigolds to keep the bugs
away. The dirt yard was swept clean as a whistle and felt cool to
our bare feet.

It was a fact that Amos always had puppies and kittens to play
with. It seemed every stray for miles around found its way to

Amos's back door. He would train the dogs to hunt and then would sell them to the local hunters for a pretty penny. When asked about all the cats he had (at one time he had about thirty), he would say, "A cat has nine lives and one day he uses the ninth life to kiss this heah world good-bye." The cats would come and go and slowly disappear one at a time until there were only a few left; then the cycle would start all over again. Amos fed them fish heads, which he always had because he fished almost every evening. On the days when there were no fish heads, the cats would go to the cotton gin and eat their weight in mice, rats, or pigeons. Amos was known, far and wide, to be kind to every living creature.

Mr. Stevens would come over to the Big House and borrow Amos about once a week. Amos was the only person who could catch Bo Stevens's Appaloosa mare. It was a mystery to everyone at the plantation how he did it. He would wiggle onto the open pasture on all fours, and in a while the horse would come over to him, allowing Amos to gently slip the rope around its neck. He would stand and lead the horse to the barn to be saddled. No one ever succeeded in catching that wild horse except Amos.

John and I wandered up on the porch, where we found five little coon dog puppies in a box. We had a handful of the puppies out on the porch when Amos appeared unexpectedly from around the side of the house. Seeing him, we both almost had strokes. John and I dropped the puppies back in the box and leaped off the porch. Amos reached out and caught us easily by our coverall straps, pulling us close to his face. His teeth were all yellow and broken from using them to untie strings, break pecans, and do a dozen other things teeth weren't meant to do. He hissed, "Well, well, what you two in such a hurry fo'? I been wantin' to visit with you two young'uns fo' quite a spell now. Jest never could get ya to come my way . . ." He growled. "Now I's got ya both!"

We began to kick and scream for dear life. Amos held us over the side of the porch with his strong arms. We swung freely, kicking the air. After what seemed like an eternity, he let go, dropping us in a heap onto the porch. We were both dazed as we sprawled on the gritty floor.

Amos turned away and said, "Well, ya'll can jest go on home now and squall and cry to Big Ruby. Ya'll ain't nothin' but two titty babies." He paused a moment, then went on, "I jest wanted to show ya'll somethin' real perdy."

We stopped in our tracks when we heard the words "titty babies" and "real perdy." The little man jumped off the porch, motioning for us to follow him. John and I dusted off our coveralls and followed him across the yard to the chicken house.

Inside the dark, smelly house, Amos reached under a fat, clucking hen and pulled out a handful of warm downy chicks. He whispered, "Did ya'll ever see anythin' so perdy?"

He let us hold the chicks, showing us how to be ever so gentle with the fluffy baby birds. After a while, he placed the chicks carefully back under the bristled hen and led us back to his porch.

The three of us were sitting quietly when we heard a dog's cry come from inside Amos's cabin. Amos broke the reverie and said, "That must be Daisy. Guess it's about time for her to be havin' her puppies."

He got up, turned to John and me, and said, "Ya'll ever seen puppies bein' born?"

We replied, "Nah, sir."

Amos said, "Well, ya'll come on in and be's real quiet and I's sho' Daisy won't mind ya'll a-watchin'."

We followed Amos just inside the door. In a box, lying on her side and panting, was a small yellow female cur dog. I began to get ready for a rainbow to appear with an angel coming down it, bringing Daisy an armful of puppies. John's eyes were as round as white china saucers as he waited for the miracle. Amos reached down and opened Daisy's back legs. To our shock and surprise, there was a puppy's head sticking out of her backside.

I turned to John, exclaiming excitedly, "Look! Daisy is shitting out puppies!"

Before long, Daisy had five wiggling puppies, which sucked

on her tits when Amos placed them at her side. After the births were over, Amos looked at our blank faces.

Scratching his head, he said, "I guess I's got some explainin' to do."

Taking us back to the porch, he explained how puppies were conceived and existed in the female dog's belly. When he finished his lesson, he slid over to the well on his padded knees. He pulled on the rope attached to a bucket and brought up a huge striped watermelon. Cutting off three large pieces, he offered us the spring-cooled melon slices, and we gobbled them down. When we had finished, Amos took the rinds and threw them into the compost bed next to his tool shed. He used the rotted vegetables and plants as fertilizer for his gardens. That was the secret to Amos's green thumb.

He pulled out his corncob pipe and settled back in his rocker, puffing and rocking. John and I were trying to wipe the sticky watermelon juice from our faces with the sleeves of our shirts when Amos said, "Ya'll more than likely be like everyone else. What ya'll wants to know? Well, go 'head ask me, ask me anythin'. If'n I can't answer it, I'll make up a lie." He laughed.

John and I looked at each other for a long time with a jillion questions going through our little minds. After a long pause, I said, "How do ya catch Bo Stevens's horse?"

The little man almost choked on his pipe. "Well, well," he said, "boy hidy, you and half the white folks in dis heah parish would like to know the answer to dat one."

"Well," I said, "ya gonna tell us or not?"

Amos sat very still for a while, then he began knocking his pipe against his rocker. He reared back in the chair and said, "The answer to dat is a big secret. Only a few colored folks round here know the answer to it. Dem dat do make their living from the secret." Looking around and speaking low, he said, "If you and John swears on a stack of Bibles and to Gawd Almighty that ya'll will never tell a living soul, I'll tell ya the secret." He chuckled, "If you did tell, we would all be locked up in the bughouse fo' sho'." Looking around again, he said softly, "Well, I'll tell ya." Some folks said Amos could see out the back of his head. "Jacob's pappy, Timba, the witch doctor, brought the secret with him from Africa when they brought him here as a slave." Amos pulled on his pockmarked chin. "Every lasting thing I know was taught to me by Jacob, and everythin' Jacob knowed was taught to him by his pappy, Timba."

The wind shifted and blew Amos's sweaty scent right into our faces. John wrinkled his flat little nose and whispered to me, "Ooh-wee, he be smellin' like a settin' peckerwood nest." We held our breaths until the wind changed again.

Amos had a very serious tone to his voice by now. "The way to make an animal yo' slave and make it do jest what ya want it to do is . . ." He stopped, lit his pipe, and went on, "Now it got to be a penned-up animal and one you feed, do ya'll understand dat?"

We replied, "Yes, sah."

He said, "It can't be no wild one, cause it works jest the opposite on one dat's wild. They's don't like the smell of humans. Ya'll understand?"

"Yes, sah," we replied.

"Dat's why a person should always wear his clothes about two weeks without changin' um fo' he puts um on a scarecrow. Get um good and human-smelling. Ya'll understand dat? Now, here comes the answer to yo' question. Every day when you goes to feed the animal youse caught and penned, you walks out into the pen and puts the feed down in front of yo' feet. Then you very quietly reach down and unbutton yo' trousers, very slowly pull out yo' peckerwood, and pee all around the animal's feed. I guarantee ya in a few weeks, the animal will want to get up in yo' lap. He be followin' ya around all love-sick like. And dat, my little chickens, is what the words 'chamber-lie' means. Do ya'll understand?"

Again we replied, "Yes, sah!"

Amos then said very quickly, "Ya'll want some snake stew and worm pie?"

"Nah, sah!" we screamed.

The three of us laughed for a long time until Amos finally said, "Ya'll better get on back to the Big House. I got me a lot of work to do fo' the sun sets. And remember, ya'll don't tell a soul."

We promised we wouldn't. From that day forward, we lost our fear of the strange little man, and he became our friend and teacher. By the time Big Ruby turned out the light in my room that same night, I thought I had figured out just how Mamma and Daddy had really gotten me. I couldn't look at them for about a week because of my embarrassment.

Tomatoes

There was a well-known saying around Dixie Roads that went like this: "There are two things money can't buy. One is true love, and the other homegrown tomatoes." It seemed that all a body would hear all summer long was, "How are ya'll's maters a-doin'?" and, "Afore I can get the green ones cornmealed and in the skillet, the sun is fryin' um right on the vine." Or, "My maters sho' could use a good rainin' on." And if it rained, you would hear, "I wish all this dad-burn rain would stop before my maters get so full of rainwater they pop open and rot."

To hear country folks talk, the weather is never just right for tomato crops. This year, though, was an exception. There was just the right balance of sun and rain to produce a bumper crop of picture-perfect, prize-winning tomatoes. From the cool wet spring when the plants began to grow and flower, until scorching hot September when the killer rays of the sun turned vines into dust, the main topic of conversation centered around the luscious red tomato.

Everyone's mouths would begin to water in early summer at the sight of the very first vine-ripened tomatoes turning deep pink in Miss Neta's patch behind her garage. The townfolk would do anything, short of killing one another or missing church, for a big juicy bite of an early "homegrowner." Thanks to Amos's green thumb and common sense, Miss Neta always had the very first homegrown tomatoes in the parish. Of course, he was handsomely rewarded for his efforts.

Amos always planted Miss Neta's starters before he planted ours and she always had the biggest, reddest, sweetest tomatoes in Dixie Roads. She was the envy of everyone in the parish, but she was also very stingy. She would hoard the precious tomatoes, tempting folks with them, and then gobble them down all by herself. After about a week of eating the highly acidic fruit, she would have to make a trip into town to Doc Parkes's office, complaining of a rash. The rash appeared in mean-looking welts that itched like the devil. Doc would tell her it was "nettle rash" and give her calamine lotion for it. He would also tell her that if she would stop wolfing down so many maters, the rash would go away. That is when she would start sharing her prize-winning crop with all her neighbors.

By the middle of the summer, everyone had tomatoes coming out of their ears, and you couldn't get rid of the damned things. Late in the cool of the night, Miss Neta would drive up to the Big House and pick up Sister Jesse for their late-night tomato deliveries. The two women would load up the back of Miss Neta's Rolls-Royce with sacks of them and sneak around in the dark to neighbors' houses, leaving the unwanted tomatoes on their steps. They would tiptoe back to the fancy car, feeling like they had done a good deed, and speed away into the summer night.

The exhausted women would return home only to find that someone had returned the favor and left sacks, boxes, and baskets of tomatoes on Miss Neta's steps. The unwanted fruit was a lot like a stray cat or puppy that someone has deposited on your doorstep, running away and forcing you to deal with the problem. You could hear a frustrated Miss Neta cry out, "What in the name of sweet Jesus are we gonna do with all these damn maters, Sister Jesse!"

Sister Jesse knew very well what she was going to do with them. Out of sheer guilt about wasting things, she would have to put them up for winter. By the end of the season, everyone was plainly tuckered out and had put up enough green and red tomatoes to feed half of Asia.

In the early summer, the juicy temptations were a bit more than John and I could bear. Tomatoes turned us into common criminals. One night, the succulent fruit lured us out of our beds. Clad only in our drawers, we raced barefoot across the dewy grass of the backyard to Miss Neta's garage. Salt-shaker in hand, we could hardly wait to take our first real bite of summer. The tomatoes were so tasty that before we realized it, we had both eaten our weight in the fruit. Somehow, the stolen, still sun-warmed tomatoes tasted better when we sat cross-legged in the cool dirt between the garden rows than they had at the supper table. Miss Neta never found out about our moonlit raid of her precious patch, but it was no secret to Amos and Big Ruby.

The next morning John and I both woke up in some kind of discomfort. We were covered from head to toe in nettle rash. Coming to get us for breakfast, Ruby discovered that our eyes were almost swollen shut and we were covered with stinging red patches. Ruby took us into the kitchen, made us take off our drawers near the sink, and bathed us down with cool well-water and baking soda. The worst part was that we had to stay inside all day out of the hot summer sun. When Amos was working in the patch that morning, he found our little footprints in the soft soil. He dropped his hoe and came across the backyard into the kitchen. Of course, we caught hell from both Amos and Ruby. We were only saved from a whipping because of the nettle rash.

Amos told us, "If ya'll hadn't been such hogs like Miss Neta, ya'll wouldn't be in the shape you is in. Ya see what happens to people who acts like hogs." He continued, "If'n I catch ya'll out in Miss Neta's patch agin, I'll have to call Sheriff Adcock and he'll lock ya'll up in Angola penitentiary."

Ruby said with a wink, "Next time ya'll decide ya want a mater in the middle of the night, least ya could do is bring me a big ole fat un." We all giggled as Amos passed her a big red tomato from his overall pocket, and the itching went away.

Amos had a hog named Fat Ester. Now, Fat Ester liked to eat everything, but her favorite food in the summer was tomatoes. Big, old, dirty Fat Ester would eat all the tomatoes that nobody wanted. That year, she had plenty. In the spring mud where Fat

Ester would do her grunties all summer long, little green tomato plants would appear, plus seedlings from everything else she had eaten the summer before. When the seedlings came up and had matured a bit, Amos would transplant them into Miss Neta's and our gardens.

Before he planted in the poor soil behind Miss Neta's garage, he prepared it with a mixture of different kinds of manure. For the tomatoes, he always used Fat Ester's manure. John and I would spend hour after hour watching him at work in the gardens — hoeing, weeding, and mashing huge green cutworms between his dirty fingers. You see, Amos never used any kind of poison on his crops. He would pick the bugs off by hand. We would watch the plants grow tall, flower, and produce a wide variety of healthy vegetables. Amos said to John and me one day, "If'n dat ole Miss Neta knew dat dese heah maters of hers come from Fat Ester's do-do, ooh-wee, we'd have to put her in the bug-house fo' sho'!" He clucked his tongue and kept hoeing.

One afternoon, Miss Neta was bored, so she went out into her lovely garden to admire all her many vegetables. Poking around next to the wall of the garage, she lifted the pungent leaves of a gigantic tomato plant to discover the largest green tomato she had ever seen in her life. She placed both her hands around it and exclaimed out loud, "Lord have mercy, this tomato is as big as my head and it is still growin'!" Neta couldn't believe her eyes. She said, "A real prize tomato just like in the garden books growing right in my backyard."

Now Miss Neta loved prizes better than she liked tomatoes. She was so excited, she ran into the house to call Nell Driver, the switchboard operator, to tell her about the prize beauty. Like every tidbit of news that went through the party-line switch-board, the news about the tomato circulated very quickly through the small town. The next morning, people found all sorts of excuses to drop by Miss Neta's. By noon, her whole backyard was full of townfolk who had come to see for them-selves the gigantic fruit.

The tomato grew and grew every day until it got so large that it had to be propped up with a pecan stick so it wouldn't touch the ground and spoil. Miss Neta's backyard became the most popular place in town. Needless to say, she enjoyed all the attention the tomato brought to her. People came from all over to see if it was really the biggest one in the world and to hang around telling all their tall tomato tales.

Through early August, the weather had been perfect for the "Big Boy," the name Miss Neta fondly called her tomato. When it was finally ripe and about to fall from the vine, Miss Neta called the Agriculture Department in Baton Rouge to have someone come up to Dixie Roads to measure and record the Big Boy for their books. She was assured that next Tuesday there would be two men on the train to Dixie Roads for just that purpose.

Tuesday finally arrived to find Sister Jesse at Miss Neta's preparing for the arrival of the measuring men from Baton Rouge. From her backyard, you could hear the eight o'clock train pulling into town. Sheriff Adcock met the official-looking men and escorted them through the little town to Miss Neta's, with everyone else in Dixie Roads following closely to watch the historic event. Mamma, Daddy, Big Ruby, John, and I arrived in Miss Neta's backyard about the same time everyone else did. John and I quickly found Amos, who was turning Miss Neta's ice-cream freezer under the shade of a yellow oleander far away from all the commotion in the yard.

We all knew that Amos was responsible for Big Boy, but not to hear Miss Neta tell it. She cavorted around the shaded yard, boasting and bragging, serving homemade peach ice cream and teacakes to all her guests. Finally, it was time to view the huge tomato. Miss Neta got everyone's attention and led the party behind the garage. Tape measure in hand, the two men from Baton Rouge bent down, removed the pecan stick, and began to measure the largest tomato they had ever seen. After many oohs and ahhs, one of the men picked Big Boy, wrapped it in a hand towel, and gave it to the other man, who was holding a hand scale. Big Boy weighed in at exactly five pounds. Gasps were heard all over the yard when the official weight was announced, and Miss Neta cried. Doc Parkes turned to Miss Neta and remarked, "Gawd dog, old Big Boy weighed in bigger than most newborn babies!" At that, Miss Neta lost all control and sobbed hysterically.

John and I noticed that poor Amos was over in the side yard looking very put-upon. John turned to me and said, "Shoot, Cotton, dat ole Big Boy ain't nearly as big as the mater dat's a-growin' down at Fat Ester's pen."

We had been watching a huge tomato that was growing along the fence post at the hog pen. John and I left all the commotion at Miss Neta's and headed toward Fat Ester's pen in a dead run. When we arrived at the pen, we sized up the huge fruit and decided without a doubt that it was much larger than Miss Neta's Big Boy. We walked around and around the tomato, trying to figure out how we could pick it and get the heavy thing back up to the yard. At this point, Jake came riding by in the goat cart. He helped us pick the huge tomato and lay it in the back of the little cart. We gave the goat a swat and headed back to Miss Neta's with the real prize tomato.

When we arrived in the backyard, John and I ran over to the two men. I said, "Mister, mister, come see what we got over heah in the cart." Hearing all the noise, everyone left Miss Neta with Big Boy in her lap and crowded around the little goat cart, their mouths agape. The men measured and weighed the tomato, announcing its weight at a little over six pounds. They both agreed that it was by far the biggest tomato they had ever seen, and it was definitely the prize tomato. Of course, the men wanted to know who had grown the monster, and we all pointed to Amos. Miss Neta shot Amos a look that would have melted steel. Amos stuttered, looked down, and began to kick the dirt with his deformed little feet. Finally he confessed nervously, "Nah, sah. I didn't grow dat ole tomato. All the glory goes to Fat Ester."

Miss Neta asked with alarm, "How could an old pig grow anything?"

John and I were the only ones who knew what Amos was talking about. Everyone went on admiring Ester's tomato, paying no attention to Miss Neta's whining. The men from Baton Rouge took a picture of the oversized fruit and recorded it in their books as "Ester's Better Boy." Then they left to meet their train.

Miss Neta didn't speak to any of us for a long time. When everyone left, Jake, Amos, John, and I pulled the goat and cart, along with Better Boy, down to Fat Ester's pen. Amos picked the big tomato out of the back of the cart and threw it across the fence for Ester to eat. We stood there watching Ester devour her squashed tomato.

Finally, Amos remarked, "Ya did good, fat pig. But see if ya can't do-do a bigger one next year, ya heah." We all waited with bated breath for the next summer's homegrown tomatoes.

Clara

She came on the scene as warm as flower-scented spring air, just as the cold gray skies of winter were giving way to warmer, sunnier days and the narcissus and daffodils were lifting their pollen-dusted faces up toward the sun.

When the red and silver bus from Shreveport stopped in front of Beason's store, Mamma and Daddy were working across the street at the cafe. Mamma checked her wristwatch and looked out the window. "Well, I'll be dogged. The bus is early for once. I wonder who it's letting off?"

Daddy asked the group of bobby-soxers in the rear booth if he could help them. One of the boys replied, "Yeah, glad dad, we'll have two Cokes and four straws and some change for the jukebox."

The two girls giggled and fluffed their newly permed hair. The girls sat on one side of the leather booth and the two boys on the other side, couples facing with their heads together. They drank from separate straws out of the same bottles, moving their legs under the table to the music.

Daddy scratched his head and remarked to Mamma, "I'll tell you, Miss Elsie, I don't know what this world is coming to. They have no respect for their elders."

Clara Touche stepped off the bus into the soft clay dirt, clutching her little handbag against her large bosom. She was dressed in a soft lilac skirt and blouse. The warm wind caught the skirt and blew it up, exposing a pair of long, shapely, honey-colored legs. Two young men dressed in navy uniforms stepped off the bus after her and started blowing wolf-whistles as she was trying to hold her dress in place. One of the sailors called, "Hey, honey, you is the cat's pajamas. I bet you can boogie-woogie under the sheets!" The other one said, "What's a classy gal like you doing in this little fleabag town?"

Mamma said as the bus pulled away, "Those fish sure are a long way from water. That high yellow gal must be the one I heard was coming to work at the Stevens's plantation."

(Amy, who worked for Mr. Stevens, kept everyone in town informed of any goings-on at the plantation. She knew all the gossip about how Clara and Mr. Stevens had met. Amy talked to anyone who would listen, including Nell Driver. Nell, in turn, kept the switchboard lit up passing the gossip along. This is Clara's story as I eventually learned it.)

Clara crossed the street to get away from the sailors, her head held high, and waited in the shade in front of the cafe. In a few minutes, another bus came along and the sailors boarded it. It took off down the dirt street, heading for the highway that ran all the way to Little Rock, Arkansas. As she waited, Clara's mind began to wander. She thought to herself about the day she had met Mr. Stevens.

★   ★   ★

He had come to New Orleans on a business trip, and the first night after his arrival he had visited the infamous Hotel de Paris. He was a tall handsome man with silver hair and a moustache — reportedly worth millions. Clara had worked in the hotel as a courtesan since she turned thirteen. Now she was twenty-eight and looked much older.

After their initial meeting and their night together, Mr. Stevens showered her with flowers and gifts. He had fallen for the beautiful Clara and was at the hotel every night for a week. When Mr. Stevens returned to Dixie Roads, he found his sickly wife, Bootsy, had become gravely ill. Bootsy died less than a month later. The day after the funeral, he sent for Clara to work at the plantation. She was to be head maid of the massive house and responsible for a few other chores that decent folks didn't talk about in broad daylight.

★ ★ ★

Clara paced back and forth in front of the cafe, first looking one way down the street and then the other. In a while, a pickup came roaring around the corner in a cloud of red dust and screeched to a halt in front of the little cafe. The door of the truck opened and out stepped a tall, thin, blond boy — Bo Stevens, Mr. Stevens's only heir.

Every other boy his age had been drafted and was fighting in World War II. All the townfolk wondered how Mr. Stevens had managed to keep Bo out of the war. Some said he had paid the government a pretty penny to keep his son home.

Bo broke into a wild, rascal smile when he saw how beautiful Clara was. He said, "Hey, you must be Clara. I'm Bo Stevens. You been here long?"

She lied and said, "No, I just got here."

He picked up her small suitcase and placed it in the back of the truck. She slid into the cab, saying, "I just brought a few things. I put my trunks on the train before I left New Orleans. They should arrive in a few days."

Bo was fascinated with her accent and said, "You sound almost like a Yankee."

She replied, "It is a well-known fact, sir, that South Louisiana folks and North Louisiana folks are as different as daylight and darkness."

The pickup moved slowly out of town toward the plantation. As they rode along, a warm breeze came through the open windows, playing in their hair. Bo said, "What a lovely day it is."

Clara agreed, "It truly is."

Pulling off the highway, the pickup crossed a cattle grate. Over the grate, a large sign read STEVENS PLANTATION. In front of them was a long oak-shaded drive bordered on either side by fields of bulbs in full bloom. Clara sat up and looked at the fields of yellow and white flowers. Deeply breathing in the fragrance, she asked, "Oh, Bo, can we stop and pick a bouquet?"

He pulled the truck to a stop under a live oak, and they both got out. Clara ran into the flowers and turned round and round like a small child. Dropping to her knees, she buried her face in the fragrant, cool flowers. She gathered an armful of narcissus and daffodils and remarked to Bo, "I like the little jonquils best. They smell so sweet. They are truly spring to me."

He couldn't get over how lovely and natural she was. He told her, "My mother had all these bulbs shipped over from Holland. They were her favorite, too." Then he turned and said, "Well, we better go or we'll be late for the crawfish boil."

Bo helped Clara and her large bouquet into the truck and slid under the wheel. She selected two big King Alfreds and placed one in her hair and one behind Bo's left ear. They both laughed as he slowly eased the pickup down the oak-canopied drive.

The truck pulled up a circular brick drive in front of the massive white antebellum house. Mr. Stevens and two colored women in starched white uniforms were waiting on the veranda. He came down the steps and opened Clara's door to help her out, exclaiming, "Clara, you are truly here! I thought you would never arrive. Oh, what beautiful flowers! You look like spring itself." He gave the flowers to one of the maids and her suitcase to the other. He said, "Amy and Dolly, this is Clara. She's going to be our new head maid."

The women curtsied and said, "Pleased to meet ya, Clara."

As they were going through the double doors, Mr. Stevens instructed, "Amy, put Clara's things in Miss Bootsy's room. And Dolly, put the flowers in some water. I'm sure Clara will want to arrange them when she gets settled. Oh, Bo, you better get on down to the levee and see how the crawfish boil is coming along and tell them that the guest of honor and I will be there shortly." He winked at his son and said, "Clara needs to rest up from her trip."

Bo pulled up to the levee and left the pickup. He was greeted by a large group of Negroes. They were field hands and house servants who lived and worked on the big farm. He walked through the crowd calling everyone's name as he passed on his way to the blazing log fires.

Bo asked, "Amos, how's everything coming?"

Amos had been in charge of catching the crawfish and gathering the young cattail shoots for the party. He and a handful of children had sieved the water of the Red River most of the day to catch the muddy critters. They had gathered the cattails along the banks of the levee.

Amos pointed to the cast-iron pot on the roaring fire and said, "Mr. Bo, we got enough crawfish and cattails to feed half the town of Dixie Roads."

Bo looked into the pot. "You did good, Amos. Mr. Stevens and Clara will be along shortly. They have some catching up to do."

Bo walked over to the banks of the river and sat down, facing the setting sun. He was thinking about what his father and Clara were doing back at the plantation. As he thought, a willowy ebony girl sprang from the shadows like a panther. She took a seat in the sand at his feet.

Surprised, Bo remarked, "Well, hey, Jemima! Where did you come from?"

"Did that yeller gal gits heah?" she asked.

Bo nodded his head.

"I guess since she is heah I be goin' back to the kitchen to work," Jemima remarked through clenched teeth.

Bo said, "Of course, you knew all along that when Clara arrived, you'd be relieved of your duties as head maid." He looked down into her face and began to smile. "Jemima, you ought to see her. She is the prettiest thing I've ever seen."

Jumping to her feet, Jemima crowed, "Well, I be gawd-damn! Maybe I's got to step down from my house duties, but I be damned if I's goin' to get out of yo' bed fo' dat bitch!"

Bo laughed, "Now, now, do I see some jealousy in those eyes? Don't worry, she belongs to the old man." He pulled her to him in an embrace, kissing her on her full lips.

By the time Mr. Stevens and Clara arrived, the pot of steaming crawfish and cattails had been dumped out on newspaper on the large wooden table and all the folks were helping themselves to the tasty treats. Mr. Stevens clapped his hands for their attention and everyone looked up.

"I would like for you all to meet Clara," he said. Everyone put down their plates and gathered around the exotic beauty from New Orleans.

Clara was the center of attention. Bo would hardly leave her side, which made Jemima mad as a wet hen. Clara told him that she knew what crawfish were and had eaten her weight in the little creatures, but she had never tried cattails.

"You just put a little salt and lemon-butter on them," Bo said.

Clara tasted one and exclaimed, "These taste sort of like asparagus!"

Jemima watched them, finally walking over to where they stood. She whispered something in Bo's ear. Reluctantly, he left Clara, saying good-night to everyone as he followed Jemima to the pickup. They got in and raced down the levee into the pitch-dark night, which was lit only by the red glow of the fires.

Mr. Stevens turned to Clara and said, "I worry about that boy. He's not happy. All his friends are off fighting the war. He's gotten so wild. He and that Jemima." He shook his head. "They're going to the Moonlite Cafe. They go there every night to get drunk and God knows what else."

Clara quickly learned her duties and did everything with a lot of class. She liked being bossy and throwing parties. She was very happy at the Stevens's plantation, at least for a while.

Then, suddenly, gossip was spreading around town like a hurricane. Ruby got hold of the news from Amy. Ruby told Jesse, Nell Driver, and Miss Neta that Mr. Stevens had come home unexpectedly one day and caught Clara and Bo in his very own bed in broad daylight. Jemima had threatened to kill Clara, and Mr. Stevens kicked her out of the house without a penny in her purse. Ruby said that Amy was surprised Mr. Stevens hadn't caught them before that particular day. Amy also told Ruby that Bo and Mr. Stevens had had a knock-down-drag-out fight right in the front yard and that Mr. Stevens had almost killed Bo. Bo had run off, and not a soul knew where he was.

"It serves Clara right," Ruby said. "Who did dat gal think she was? Comin' up heah from New Orleans and causin' all dis trouble and hoppin' from one bed to the other. I hope she takes her yeller-lookin' self back to New Orleans."

Clara appeared at our back door one afternoon during our quiet period after lunch. I was still in the kitchen with Big Ruby and Sister Jesse. I will never forget how beautiful Clara was. She was dressed in lilac with an adornment of ivory jewelry on her arms, neck, and ears. Her coarse black hair was piled high on her head in a forties style. The blackness of her hair contrasted vividly with her skin, which was the color of bruised magnolia petals. Her lips and cheeks were tinted red. A strong smell of cologne and talc floated through the kitchen air.

Ruby and Jesse were in the midst of their chores when the young woman appeared. Big Ruby got up to answer the knock while Sister Jesse continued to shell peas.

"What you want round heah, gal?" Ruby asked. She and the young woman were as different as daylight and darkness.

"I heard ya'll might need some help around here," she replied.

"Ya'll hafta talk to the mistress of the house."

"When might she be home?"

"You can never tell," said Ruby, "but ya might catch her down to the cafe on Main Street."

The young woman murmured "Thank you" as she turned to leave. Clutching her little handbag, she teetered on her high heels down the gravel drive.

Big Ruby headed back to the table to help Sister Jesse finish shelling peas.

"Who was dat high yeller gal?" asked Jesse.

"My Gawd! Dat was Clara! What in the world is she showin' up at our backdoor fo'? Mr. Stevens let her go cause dey say . . ." Ruby's large black eyes looked around as she said in a whisper, "Dey say she took up with the young Stevens boy, Bo."

"I declare! Is dat a fact?" said Jesse.

"Um huh, folks say she be tryin' to make some money to git a bus ticket back to New Orleans."

Mamma came in the next day with big news.

"I've got a surprise for ya'll. Being that Auntie Mary's ailing and canning season is upon us, I've hired a girl to help out. Sister Jesse can take care of Auntie Mary's needs, and Big Ruby can put up all the fruits and vegetables. The new girl, Clara, can take care of Cotton."

"Clara!" wailed Big Ruby. I detected a note of disapproval in her voice.

"Yes, Clara. She'll be here this afternoon for ya'll to break in. I've got to go up to the cafe in Ida and won't be back until tomorrow. Oh, by the way, she'll be staying in Amos's house. I have spoken to Miss Neta and she said Amos can stay in her guest house for the time being. I have a feeling Clara won't be here long."

That afternoon, Bo Stevens's pickup pulled up the drive. Clara got out with two suitcases made of cardboard and a big paper sack.

Ruby saw her coming and said, "Would ya look at dat! Bo with dat girl in broad daylight."

She turned to me. "Cotton, go meet Clara and take her down to Amos's cabin," she ordered. "I don't know what dis world's comin' to . . . ain't got no shame, dat gal."

"Hi-do," I said as I ran up to Clara with a little bow.

"Oh, what a fine little soul! You are a sugar cube. You must be Cotton Candy. I'm Clara, and you and me is gonna get along just fine."

She didn't talk like the rest of the Negroes I knew. For that matter, nothing about her was the same. Sister Jesse said she had an air about her that was like an African queen.

★   ★   ★

One hot, lazy afternoon, Ruby stopped me and said, "I don't see you much anymo'. What you be doin' all dis time?"

It was true. Since Clara had come, I was down at her house most of the time. She would dress me in her clothes and jewelry. She let me wear her makeup and she would even spray cologne on me. The stories she told me were like none I had ever heard before. Oh, how I loved her! She was so beautiful, with her low, soothing voice.

Late one day I came home from playing with Clara, still wearing a lipstick smear and reeking of cologne. Ruby grabbed me as I ran through the door.

"Cotton! What has ya'll been doin' down there? Look at yo' face! You smell like a cheap ho' in church. Dat yeller witch from New Orleans has put a spell on my baby!"

Tears welled in Ruby's wide black eyes, and I knew I had hurt her deeply. But I knew she was right about Clara's spell: I would do anything to please her!

The next evening everyone except Clara went to Miss Neta's to help her get ready for the annual Daughters of the Confederacy social meeting. I couldn't keep my mind off Clara. I kept wondering what she was doing at her house. The minute I realized that no one was paying any attention to me, I sneaked away and started for Clara's. John followed me part of the way but stopped as soon as he realized where I was going.

As I stepped on Clara's porch, I heard her singing softly. When I knocked, she came to the door.

"Cotton, honey? What's ya doin' out here on the porch?"

As I entered the cool shotgun, the special fragrance of Clara overcame me. She handed me a lace fan, and I twirled around fanning myself mockingly. Clara squealed with delight at my performance.

"Cotton? Did you ever think about doin' somethin' dangerous?"

I put the fan aside and sat next to her on the bed. I was breathless.

"Yes'm . . . I guess so."

Clara was very excited. After I responded, she lunged for me and said, "I mean really wild and crazy! Dangerous and wild!" My heart was pounding in my throat as Clara hissed in my ear. "Let's sneak off. Nobody will ever know. Ever'body's worried with Miss Neta and her 'ciety party tonight!"

She took me by the hand and led me into the night, past the row of shotgun houses to the dirt road. We turned left, cut across the cotton fields and hit the railroad tracks. As we walked in the middle of the crossties, I thought we were headed for town. But we weren't. Instead, we left the tracks and followed a cow path to a run-down shanty house.

Signs were posted all over the front of the shanty. A bunch of Negro men were sitting on the porch drinking beer. As we climbed the steps, everyone tipped their hats and greeted us. We entered through a fly-covered screen door. The place was dark and smelled of smoke, stale beer, and cheap wine. A huge electric fan buzzed in the corner.

In the middle of the room stood a long shaky bar. At the end of it sat Bo Stevens drinking beer with a girl as black as midnight. He looked up at Clara and me, and quickly left the girl to come to us. I recognized her. She was Jemima.

"Hi," Bo said softly, gazing at Clara.

He picked me up and sat me on top of the shaky bar. Clara sat on a stool, glaring at Jemima, while Bo bought me a Grapette and a bag of peanuts. Clara ordered a Coca-Cola and Bo ordered a beer. After the drinks arrived, the two began speaking in hushed whispers.

I looked around the dark room. A jukebox with colored lights sat in one corner. An old colored gentleman, Doctor Theophrastus, put some money into it and the lights began to dance as "Sweet Georgia Brown" blared out. The old man started to move in a slow, rotating fashion. I was mesmerized.

"What's he doing?" I asked, barely containing my excitement.

"Cotton, honey, he's doin' the shuffle — or the be-bop, as the white folks say. Why don't you try it, sugar?" Clara teased.

I jumped off the bar and started to imitate him. After a while, I looked just like him! Everyone clapped and laughed, encouraging me even more.

I danced all evening, picking up a handful of pennies. When we were ready to leave, I was full of Grapette, peanuts, and dance. Everyone waved good-bye and told me to come back anytime.

Doctor Theophrastus took my small white hand in his and said, "Youse got the Saint Vitus in ya. Keep dancin'. It's good for yo' soul!"

He released my hand as he clicked his heels. Then he bowed and tipped his hat and turned to put another nickel in the jukebox. Bo told Clara that he would come by her shotgun later, when it was dark, to pick her up.

As we walked home, Clara told me to keep "hushed" about being at the Moonlite Cafe, or we would both be in a lot of trouble. I didn't understand why. I had had such a good time. Later that night, as I lay in bed with a tummy ache, I thought about how much I loved Clara. The house grew dark and still as the night crept on.

Dozing off to sleep, I saw a reflection of light cross my ceiling. It was Bo's pickup truck. Clara's front screen door opened, then slammed closed again. The truck sped away into the night.

The next day I woke feeling much better than I had the night before. I dressed and went into the kitchen, where Big Ruby and Sister Jesse were sitting quietly at the table having their morning coffee. There was a knock at the back door, and Big Ruby shuffled over to open it. To our surprise, it was Sheriff Adcock. "I came to inquire about a Miss Clara," he said. I couldn't understand what else he was saying.

Ruby began to holler and cried, "Oh, Lord! Oh, Lord, no!"

She stood there rocking back and forth in a state of disbelief. The sheriff thanked her and quickly left. Sister Jesse got up to help Ruby to the table.

"What in sweet Jesus name is wrong?" she asked.

Ruby clutched her breast and cried, "They kilt Clara!"

"What? Who?" moaned Sister Jesse. I was struck dumb.

"Jemima Jones . . . Seems that Bo and Clara went to the Moonlite Cafe last night," Ruby explained tearfully. "Jemima picked a fight with Clara over Bo. She cut Clara's pretty throat from ear to ear. Kilt her dead!"

I couldn't believe it! My beautiful Clara would never be back!

Ruby continued, "Sheriff got Jemima locked in the jailhouse. Says she's wild as a tiger possessed by the devil . . . says the electric chair is comin' from Shreeport. They's gonna teach us all a lesson and electrocute her 'fore she can squeal on Bo." Ruby hung her head down and cried.

We didn't see Bo anymore after Clara's death. Some said that the sheriff rushed him out of Dixie Roads. Rumor had it that he was in the army.

In time I learned that these kinds of things were part of our North Louisiana way of life in the forties. But then I only knew that Clara was gone forever.

The Passin' of Auntie Mary

Dixie Roads didn't have a mortuary for colored folks. The Saint Rest Funeral Home had been closed down by the sheriff over two years ago because of a scandal. Ruby said it went something like this.

★ ★ ★

Dr. Washington was the mortician in town. He and his wife, Elvira, ran the little establishment with the help of their teenage daughter, Vashtie, who had a whole lot more than most of the Negro girls in her school and wanted for practically nothing. The one thing she was lacking, though, was looks. When Ruby passed Vashtie on the street, she would say, "Po' chile, she be so ugly she could haunt a house."

One cold and snowy February day, just before Valentine's, Artis Jackson asked Vashtie for a date to the Valentine's dance at their school. Now he was no prize either. "He could have stopped ten clocks," Ruby chuckled.

Mrs. Washington was a busy woman. Running from the mortuary, located in the back of their house, to her motherly duties in the front of their house wore her out! She said to Vashtie, "I don't know what we's gonna do. I ain't got time nor money to make you a new dress on such short notice. 'Sides, I has to help yo' pappy get a body ready for display."

Vashtie began to bawl, and her mother said, "Now hush

squallin', honey." But Vashtie had her mind set on a new red dress for the dance.

"I know what I'll do," Mrs. Washington remarked as she pulled a white dress out of her own closet. "This heah is my new Sunday dress. I'll take it up here and there and we'll dye it red." Vashtie dried her pitiful eyes.

It took three gallons of red dye to color the dress. Mrs. Washington worked on it all morning, It began to snow around noon and by the time she had finished, the ground was covered with a foot of snow and it was pitch dark. She opened the back door and threw the three gallons of red dye out beside the house. Then she put on her coat, and walked through the snow to the clothesline, and hung up the dress, hoping that the sun would come out in the morning and dry it. She went back inside and went to bed.

Early the next morning, Miss Neta passed the Washingtons' in her fancy car. Nosy as she was, she did not fail to see the red dye in the white snow and the red dress hanging on the clothesline. She almost fainted at the wheel. She put that fine car in high gear and high-tailed it home, ran immediately to the telephone, and rang up Nell Driver, the switchboard operator.

"Nell, honey, those niggers down at the Washingtons' funeral home are throwing buckets of blood right out the back door of the place and hanging bloody rags out to dry!"

Nell said, "Neta, honey, I'll call you right back. You are at home, aren't you, sweetness?"

Of course, it didn't take Nell long to pass the news all over the little town.

By noon, strange things began to happen over at the Washingtons'. First, the Simms family came with a hearse from a funeral home in Shreveport, got the body of old Martha Simms, and took off toward Shreveport without a word. Then Artis Jackson called Vashtie and broke his date with her without an explanation. You could hear Vashtie squalling all over town. Later, Sheriff Adcock came by, saw the red stuff in the snow, puked beside his car, and tacked a quarantine sign to the front door.

Sheriff told the Washingtons he was closing down the funeral home for sanitary reasons and they had better get out of town before they got "kilt." By the time they had packed their belongings into the big hearse, the snow had melted and the dye had disappeared.

"The po' souls never knew what happened," Ruby finished, shaking her head, as we all went to bed.

★   ★   ★

The next day began as usual, with everyone coming to the Big House for breakfast. When heads were counted by Sister and Big Ruby, they found that Auntie Mary hadn't shown up.

Sister Jesse told Ruby, "I better go on down and see about Auntie. She ain't been feeling good lately. I worry about her so. She be so po' lookin'."

Sister fixed a plate of food and headed out the back door to Auntie Mary's. In a few minutes, we heard a blood-curdling scream coming from Auntie's little house. Ruby dropped the wooden spoon in the grits, stepped in her slides, and ran toward the whitewashed house. John and I ran out after her.

Amos, Jewel, John, and I arrived about the same time on the porch of Auntie's house. From inside we could hear Sister and Ruby crying and hollering. We waited a short time; then Sister Jesse came out to us.

"Po' Mary has passed!" she wailed.

John and I were instructed to run home and tell Mamma and Daddy. On the way, I asked John what "passed" meant. He looked at me with his big round eyes and said, "When you die, you pass from one life to another with Gawd."

We followed Mamma and Daddy back to Auntie's. We were told to stay put on the porch while the grown-ups entered the dark house. In a while, everyone except Ruby left Auntie's house to return to the Big House. John and I stayed on the porch. After everyone was out of sight, we went to the screen and peered inside. There was Ruby kneeling beside Auntie's bed, hands folded, head down, crying and talking to her as if she was still alive.

"Oh, Auntie, I'm sorry I lied to you . . . and maybe I could have been better to you," Ruby moaned.

All of a sudden, we heard a hiss, just like when you let air out of a bicycle tire, and there was Auntie Mary sitting straight up in bed. John and I were petrified. Ruby raised her head and froze in the middle of her prayer. Then she jumped to her feet and began to shake all over in a spastic fit, stamping her feet as she shook. When her feet were able to move, she ran screaming onto the porch, knocking us to the ground. As she raced to the Big House, she fell and rolled in the grass a couple of times.

The following day, the ice man arrived early with a huge amount of ice. By now, Ruby had partially recovered from Auntie Mary's rising. (It took a handful of colored men to lay Auntie back on her bed.) I decided to risk asking Ruby why they needed all the ice.

"Being that it's hot summertime and we don't have a Negro funeral home, dey gonna hafta put Mary on ice till all her relatives can come and view the body," she answered.

Auntie lay on ice for a week and a half in her hot little house. Every day, the ice man came with his delivery. Pretty soon, the whole front yard was flooded. The folks that came to see Auntie had to avoid the mud, water, and yellowed cape jasmine, which was used to mask the smell.

After the service, Ruby and Jesse were completely tuckered out. Later, when they had rested, we all met in the kitchen for a snack. Jesse, Ruby, and I sat around the big table. For a long time, no one said a word. Suddenly, Jesse started snickering, and before long we were all laughing, really not knowing why.

When the spontaneous laughter subsided, Jesse wove her tale about the long day at the funeral. It seems that after the hearse pulled out of the yard and headed toward the New Light Baptist Church, everything started going wrong. The procession had to go miles into the country to the church, which was located in the middle of a hot, dusty cotton field.

When they arrived at the little church, the top of the hearse was covered with buzzards. Mary had been on ice too long. The preacher had to get his gun to get rid of the pests.

The service lasted all day, with eulogies to Auntie Mary between greens and potato salads. Then, in the middle of a thunderstorm, the whole church moved out to the cemetery for the laying in the earth. The preacher had to say a few more words on behalf of the deceased before the small wooden casket could finally be lowered into the hole in the ground. Everyone passed by to look in the grave. Jesse and Ruby were last. Jesse leaned over, said a few words, threw a tea rose into the pit and walked away. Ruby also stepped to the side of the grave, but she got too close. She slipped and slid and, clawing the wet earth, fell into the grave, landing on top of the casket. Everyone ran over to peer down at her.

Jesse turned to the astounded preacher and said, "Don't bother to take her out. Jest cover um both up. Cause when you git dat fat woman out, she won't be worth shootin'. 'Sides, she's scared to death of dead folks."

We laughed heartily for a long time.

When Ruby put me to bed, she said, "Well, I guess Sister Jesse's story relieved all the tension. Laughin' is good medicine. Don't ever forget it, chile." She picked the dried mud from under her fingernails with a toothpick.

Theophrastus,
the Doctor of Dance

Amos came to the back door the Friday morning after Auntie Mary's funeral. Ruby went over to the screen to see what he wanted.

"What's the matter, Amos? Didn't you get enough breakfast dis mornin'? Don't tell me you wants some more biscuits and ribbon cane syrup."

"Nah, I's had a-plenty. I's jest wonderin' if you might let Cotton and John go a-fishin' with me? I's goin' over to Mr. Stevens's pond. I heah the fish is walkin' out of the water and jumpin' in yo' sack."

They both laughed. John and I were sitting in the middle of the floor playing with our pet frog, Luther.

Jesse piped in, pointing to the big bullfrog, "Let um go, Ruby. I can't do my work with dat thing loose in here."

"I guess it'll be all right, if you promise to watch um like a hawk and have um back by suppertime," Ruby decided. She also reminded him that neither of us could swim.

We put Luther in a shoe box and followed Amos to the garage where he picked up three cane poles. Then we followed him to his house where he had Bill, the goat, hitched to the faded gold cart. He put us in the cart and turned the goat onto the dirt road. We rolled across the cotton fields up to the railroad tracks, where we got out to pull the cart across the steel bars. On the other side, we followed a cow trail that passed in front of the Moonlite Cafe.

I thought of the day Clara and I had sneaked away from Miss Neta's, and tried to hide my tears from Amos and John.

Not missing a trick, John asked, "What is got into you, Cotton?"

"I got an ole gnat in my eye," I lied.

We climbed a small clay hill and came upon an orange pond shimmering in the sun.

As we got closer, Amos said, "It look like somebody is already a-fishin' down there."

We pulled the goat cart up to the bank and tied Bill to a cypress stump. Theophrastus was sitting on a lard can with his cane pole dangling in the reddish-brown water.

He tipped his hat with the colorful feathers in the band and said, "Hey, Amos, you better get to fishin' 'fore I catch all of um." He reached down and pulled a long string of perch and bream out of the muddy water. Returning the fish to the water, he asked, "Who's that with ya?"

It's jest Cotton and John. I'm gonna teach um how to fish," Amos replied.

"Oh, I know who they is. I's seen the little parade on Sattidy, and Cotton and I go a ways back, don't we, chile?" said the Doctor.

"Yes, sah," I said.

Memories of the trip Clara and I had made to the Moonlite Cafe, of how we had all danced together and the fun we had had, made me miss Clara even more!

Theophrastus broke the silence, "Cotton, you been practicin' the foot work I showed ya?"

I said, "Yes, sah," and to the amazement of John and Amos, I broke into the dance he had taught me on that ill-fated day.

Amos showed John and me how to line and weight the cane poles and how to hook the wiggling worms. John and Amos sat on the bank together while I sat next to Doctor Theophrastus.

After a while, I asked quietly, "How did you learn to dance like that?"

The Doctor pushed his hat to the back of his gray head and said, "Chile, that is a long story." He grinned his toothless grin.

"I was born in the late 1800s to African slave parents on the Cypress Grove Plantation. Everyone says I came out of my mammy dancin'. Mammy would sing to me and tap out rhythm on the sides of my wooden cradle. They say my little feet jiggled around keeping time with the rhythms. In no time I was on my feet imitating them sounds on the sandy floor. A-woosh, chitty to chitty, slide and glide." He got up and began to dance. "I guess I musta heard them sounds while still in my mammy's belly.

"By the time I was yo' age, I had talked the blacksmith into making me some iron taps for my shoes." He winked at me and said, "So I's could hear them rhythms better and they'd be clearer to the folks I was a-entertainin'. Sounded jest like a horse on a cobblestone street, clack-a-de-clack, clack.

"I used to dance at all the colored weddings and parties. The boss would call me up to the plantation house from the quarters to dance fo' the white folks' parties. He would say, 'Theophrastus, I want you to dance fo' yo' supper.'" He slapped his knees and giggled. "I was loaned out to the other plantations to perform at the big parties. The white folks like my dancin' so much, they'd throw pennies and nickels, and one time I even got a dime. I figured they's so drunk, they thought the dime was a penny . . . Now, where was I? Oh, before long I had a little tobacco sack full of money." He stopped. "You know, chile, a penny would buy a lot in them days.

"My mammy and pappy were gettin' ole and whipped down. One night I heard a train comin' down the tracks. The sound of that there train made me want to get up and go. So I did. I ran inside, got my coat and money sack, and jumped the train, leavin' my mammy and pappy behind." He turned and pointed to the train tracks. "It was right over there where I jumped that freight."

We both caught a fish at the same time. It was the first fish I'd ever caught, and I felt sorry for it.

Putting the fish on the string, the Doctor continued, "I went all the way to Kansas City in a boxcar with a handful of young Negro boys who had the same idea as me. After a few days, my money was gettin' low. I had this heah idea." He pointed to his noggin. "If the white folks at the plantation would throw money at me, so would the people in Kansas City. I found myself a busy street corner, turned my hat up, and began to dance. To my surprise, I made a quarter. The next day, I went to that same corner and danced up a storm. In no time, I had an audience. The white folks were a-clappin' and laughin' when all of a sudden out of the crowd came a fat black man dressed fit to kill. He said, 'Rastus, I'd like to talk to you.' He introduced himself as Doctor Billy and told me he had a tent show on the outskirts of town called the 'Doctor Billy Medicine Show.' He had a fine one-horse buggy. We both got in it and headed south of town to the tent show.

"When we got there, we went into his office and he offered me a shot of his medicine. It was nothin' more than corn liquor. We laughed. Doctor Billy said, 'I have this high yeller gal that works for me that needs a dancin' partner. Would you be interested?' Almost down to my last penny, tired of dancin' on the streets, and two shots of Billy's magic potion in my belly, I said I would. Feeling the whiskey had made me frisky. I said, 'Where is this gal?' He said, 'You can't see her until tomorrow. Now you go on and get yo' things and be back here at eight o'clock in the morning to practice with her.' I went back to the hobo camp where I had been stayin'. In the morning, I said good-bye to the boys, got my few belongins, and walked back to the tent show, arrivin' right on time.

"I found Doctor Billy over in the main tent. He introduced me to the most beautiful lady I ever seen in my life. He called her Diedra Sizemore. She was otherwise known as the lovely Clair St. James. I was speechless. Doctor Billy said, 'I'll be back in an hour to see how you two are gettin' along.' When he was gone, I got up on the little wooden stage, felt my way around, never being on a real stage before. I started tapping out some rhythms. The taps say hap-hap-hap-H-A-P-P-Y, happy happy hap-hap, imitating the sounds of the taps with my mouth. The rhythms were intoxicating to her, and before long, Miss St. James was up by my side imitating my every move. We danced till we were about to drop in our tracks. I'd throw a step at her and she'd pick it up and then she'd throw one at me. Finally, I grabbed her in my arms, twirled her round and round till we were dizzy and madly in love. Doctor Billy came back and asked, 'Well, how ya'll doin'?' He could see the joy on both our faces and said, 'Ya'll did jest fine.' Clair said, 'Oh, Billy, he is truly my doctor. He makes me feel so good. He is my doctor of dance.' And that's how I got the name Doctor Theophrastus.

"We left with the little tent show on a tour of the South. We went to St. Louis and then over to Atlanta, Georgia. We had new costumes made and every week or so we would change the routines. Slowly we started adding a chorus, we would pick up talented young colored children along the way, who were jest like me—they had the Saint Vitus in um.

"By the time we reached New Orleans, we had five dance numbers featuring Miss Lilly St. Clair. Doctor Billy had decided to change her name and the name of the show before we got to New Orleans. The show was now called 'Miss Lilly's All Colored Review.' He said, 'We need to be classy to play to New Orleans.'

"The crowds were completely mesmerized by the beauty of this young, light-skinned girl. In no time, Miss Lilly was the toast of New Orleans. Things kept changin'. I was no longer her partner. I picked up a young colored boy in Atlanta and trained him to take my place, because I was on the billin' as a soloist and choreographer. In smaller letters, under Miss Lilly St. Clair, appeared, 'Also Starring Doctor Theophrastus, the Doctor of Dance.' I didn't know it at the time, but I done made a bad mistake in hiring Scooter Lee, the boy dancer. Youse don't know what a dog eats till it comes out.

"The twenties came roarin' in—prohibition, new dances, underground clubs, bathtub gin . . . Doctor Billy sold the tent show, and we moved into a speakeasy in the old colored section of the French Quarter. We performed two shows a night and three on Saturdays.

"In June, on a dark and steamy night, Miss Lilly was shot to death in her dressing room by Scooter Lee, who was all liquored-up and in a jealous rage. After the funeral, I went back to Kansas City, half-mad with grief. I became the choreographer for an all-colored review called 'Harlem in Havana.' We toured with state fairs and small carnivals. One time we even played New York City." The Doctor had a gleam in his eye when he said this, but his expression changed again, quickly.

"You know, I never did get over Miss Lilly. After years on the road, we came to Shreveport to play the state fair. I took the train to Dixie Roads to find my mammy still alive, but real sick. I jest couldn't leave her that-a-way and so I got me a job at the cotton gin and paid her doctor bills. In a few years, she passed. By then, I was too old and tired to leave again. Now the only dancin' I do is at the Moonlite Cafe. I dance fo' wine now instead of pennies. It's the only thing that makes me forget Miss Lilly and the past."

By now, the man was crying in earnest. We sat there silently for a long time. In a while, Doctor Theophrastus pulled in another fish and began to laugh.

We had caught so many fish, Amos asked the Doctor over for supper. That night we had a fish fry in a black cast-iron pot in Amos's yard. All of us sat around the fire listening to Doctor Theophrastus weave his stories. As he talked, I noticed that he sipped his wine with great relish as he savored the memories he shared with us.

The War Comes to Dixie Roads

One hot sizzling August day turned into another, with everyone staying inside in front of the swamp cooler and under the ceiling fans, trying to stay cool and wishing for something to happen.

That day began very much like any other. Mamma and I spent most of the morning at the Methodist Church across the road from the Big House. All the white ladies in town would meet in the ivy-covered brick church Monday through Friday mornings to make and roll bandages for the war effort. World War II was raging and it was on everyone's minds since each of the ladies had a loved one fighting somewhere on foreign soil. There were very few young men left in the little cotton town, and the women were very nervous and insecure without their men around.

At noontime, Mamma took me back to the Big House where Daddy was waiting in the yard for us.

"Shake a leg, Miss Elsie. We've got to hurry or we'll never get there before dark," Daddy said.

He picked me up, and we entered the house through the French doors. We went through the cool dark house into the bright kitchen. Sister Jesse and Big Ruby were sitting at the table, each with a knife, eating cantaloupe. Mamma explained to them that she and Daddy had to go to Ida to work in the cafe there. Since they were going to be gone for a week, she had made a long list of things for everyone to do while they were away.

Mamma and Daddy headed out the back door to where the car sat, already running, saying, "Cotton, you be good now, and Ruby, you take care of everything heah. We'll see ya'll in a week."

Waving, they backed down the gravel drive and drove off toward Ida.

After our noon meal and naps, John and I headed for the fig tree to play. We left Jesse puttering around the kitchen and Ruby and Jewel hanging out wet clothes on the line in the backyard.

Suddenly, all hell broke loose! Down the gravel drive came two army trucks spewing gravel into the yard and disturbing our quietness. Four men dressed in uniforms jumped from the moving trucks and ran toward our front door. Seeing the strangers, Ruby and Jewel dropped the wet clothes and ran to the fig tree. They jerked John and me off the ground and ran with us to the back door. At the same moment we came through the door, the soldiers entered our kitchen through the front. Jesse dropped the dish she was drying and it shattered on the floor.

We huddled together in a small group facing the four soldiers in full combat uniform.

"Well, well, what do we have here?" asked one of the soldiers.

They moved forward with rifles in hand, bunching us against the sink.

"Four niggers and a white child," another of the soldiers answered. "Where are the owners of this ole house?"

John and I were hugging Ruby's legs so tightly that she couldn't move. Jesse held Jewel's neck, hugging her for dear life.

"Answer me!" shouted the soldier.

Ruby stepped forward, brushing John and me away. She was shaking like a leaf in a windstorm. One of the soldiers stopped her by placing his gun across her chest.

"They's gone to Ida," she barely managed to say.

"What did she say?" asked one of the men.

"I don't know. I can't understand her," replied another as he shrugged his shoulders.

"What kind of talk is that?" asked a third.

"I think she said they've gone out of town."

"Well, it doesn't really matter," the leader of the men said. "We are here to inform you that this house and its surroundings have been captured and will be used as military headquarters. All of you are our prisoners."

All the commotion brought Nell Driver across the yard to see what was happening. Two of the armed men met her at the back door. When they found out she had the switchboard, they escorted her home and disappeared into her house.

Jewel looked out the kitchen window to see two other men with guns pushing Jake and Amos up Miss Neta's back steps. They, too, disappeared. In a few minutes, we heard a blood-curdling scream from Miss Neta's place.

At that point, we children became hysterical. The soldiers grouped us all together and made us walk in front of them up the winding stairs to the door of Mamma's and Daddy's bedroom. They opened the door and shoved us inside.

"Now you lay low and be quiet. Don't turn on any lights," ordered one of the men. They locked the door from the outside. John and I stared at Big Ruby for an explanation and began to cry.

"Sweet Jesus word! Who would've thought the war would come to Dixie Roads?" Ruby gasped.

"Ya'll hush now. Hush! We's got to think," said Jesse.

She walked to the lace-curtained windows, pushed them aside, pulled the shade up just a smidgen and peered down into the backyard. She gasped. We ran over and looked down at tents, soldiers, jeeps, and tanks. Our backyard had been turned into an army camp.

"The world is comin' to an end!" moaned Ruby. We collapsed in a heap on the polished oak floor.

At dusk, the door of the bedroom opened, and a different soldier came strutting into the room. He looked older than the other men, and he had on a different uniform. He walked over to the huddle on the floor.

"I am Major Perkins, the commanding officer. That means I am the big boss. The other officer and I are getting mighty hungry. You and you," he said, pointing to Big Ruby and Sister Jesse, "follow me." Startled, the two women got off the floor and followed the officer out the door.

"Ya'll do as you are told an' don't cause no trouble or they might shoot ya," Ruby ordered as she closed the door behind her.

"You reckon they's Japs or Krauts?" John asked.

"Well, one thing fo' sho', they's not from round heah. Ya'll hear the way they talks?" Jewel remarked.

In a little while, Ruby returned to the bedroom with a plate of food for us. "Now ya'll eats this heah to keep up yo' strength. They's not a bad sort. They sho' likes to eat. They said we can carry on like they's not even heah." Then Ruby turned to Jewel, "Jesse is down in the kitchen washin' dishes. So, Jewel, we need to get those clothes in 'fore the dew falls and they's sour on the line."

Jewel looked at Big Ruby fearfully and said, "Mamma, I's don't want to go out in the backyard. It's dark and them soldier men has guns and . . ."

"Sounds like a thousand whys to me. Now let's go!" Ruby interrupted, jerking Jewel off the bed. "John, you and Cotton stay up heah out of the way."

Jewel was only twelve, but she looked much older. Her brother, Jake, teased her unmercifully about the way she looked. He would say, "If I had two mules with behinds that broad, I wouldn't take a hundred dollars apiece for um."

When they arrived in the kitchen, Ruby handed Jewel the laundry basket. "Now hurry up 'fore the sun goes down completely!" she ordered.

Jewel pushed open the screen door, balancing the basket on her hip. She walked down the steps, moving directly through the group of soldiers toward the clothesline. The backyard came alive as the men saw her. They began whistling and catcalling. Two young soldiers moved up behind her, trying to sweet-talk the nervous Jewel. One of them grabbed for her. She dropped the basket, slapping at the men, trying to protect herself. They grabbed her again, and pulled her, screaming and struggling, into the dark garage.

John and I witnessed the entire incident from the bedroom window. I raced out of the bedroom and down the stairs to the kitchen where Jesse and Ruby were working. They were so busy, they hadn't heard Jewel's cries for help.

"They's got Jewel!" I bellowed at a startled Ruby. "Two men got her and they's put her in the garage!" She grabbed her wooden spoon and flew out the door, jumping the steps. She slipped and hit the yard, landing on her rump. She struggled to her feet and continued running for the garage.

"Here comes old mamma hen with blood in her eyes! Ya'll better get out that garage! Let her go! Here she comes!" yelled the other soldiers left in the yard.

In a split second, the two soldiers piled out of the garage with their pants around their ankles. Ruby came right after them, beating them on their heads with her wooden spoon.

The soldiers disappeared into an open tent. Ruby ran back to the garage. In a few minutes, she reappeared, holding a hysterical Jewel.

Ruby walked Jewel, who was half-naked, across the backyard, desperately trying to cover her daughter with the hem of her dress.

"Oh, sir, look what they's done to my baby! They's hurt her real bad!" Ruby cried as she entered the kitchen.

"That's enough of all that screaming and hollering! Can't you see we are trying to eat supper? Now ya'll get on back upstairs and don't come out until we call you. Now get!" ordered one of the officers.

As we left the kitchen, I heard the other man say, "That gal asked for what she got. Did you see how she was built?" He continued to suck on a stew bone.

Reaching the bedroom, Jesse and Ruby laid Jewel down on the bed and tried to calm her. They stroked her face and head, talking to her in soothing tones. Jesse fetched a wet towel from the bathroom and began washing the blood from Jewel's legs. I couldn't figure out where the blood was coming from since it appeared that Jewel had not been cut in any way.

"How bad is she hurt? Oh, my baby! Hush, hon! Hush, now!" Ruby cried.

"She don't look too bad," replied Jesse, as she finished wiping away the blood.

"I's so sorry, honey. I's so ashamed. Please, forgive me for sendin' you out there to git them clothes. Mamma's so sorry!" Ruby sobbed as she held Jewel in her big, safe arms.

Jewel eventually calmed down and drifted off to sleep in my mamma's and daddy's bed. Jesse and Ruby made John and me get on the floor in a small circle and close our eyes tightly. We knelt in that small circle, praying, for most of the night.

In the dark bedroom, shadows danced around as the sounds of aircraft and muffled voices filled our fretful sleep. Searchlights crisscrossed the wallpapered ceiling.

The morning brought even worse noises. We were startled out of sleep at dawn by gunfire and low-flying planes, which dropped bombs that produced red and yellow smoke. Frightened beyond belief, we crawled under the bed and lay there, just waiting to die.

The bedroom door flew open and we heard gunfire that seemed closer than before. Two soldiers ran into the room. Jumping over the bed, they ran to the window and threw out a rope ladder. As they climbed down into the backyard, two more men followed them in hot pursuit.

Terrified, we stayed in our hiding place all morning. Every time another bomb exploded, John and I would cry.

Around eleven o'clock, everything became deadly quiet. In a while, a soldier entered the room once again. "We knew where you were," he told us as he peered under the bed. "You can come out now. The war is over. The enemy has surrendered. I am to escort you to the kitchen. The general wants to talk to you."

We crawled from our hiding place and followed the soldier to the kitchen. Standing by the back door was a tall man dressed in a uniform plastered with medals and ribbons.

"Hello, my name is General Wilson of the Red Team. We have beat the shit out of the Blue Team bastards!" he boasted.

Through red, swollen eyes, we looked at each other and then back at him for an explanation.

Seeing our tear-stained faces, he said, "I guess you all knew that this was just a war game. You know, a maneuver. Well, everything is over now. We'll be pulling out in a while with our men and artillery to head back to Bossier City and Barksdale Air Force Base. I truly hope we haven't caused you too much trouble and inconvenience. In a few days, a man will be sent over here to make a list of damages we might have made, and the U.S. government will send you a check to cover them. Thank you for your fine Southern hospitality," he said as he left.

When the last jeepload of men pulled out, we all wandered, one at a time, into the front yard. Ruby, John, Jesse, Nell Driver and her two kids, Miss Neta, Jake, Amos, Jewel, and I stood together, half-dazed and still shaking.

Five months later, Jewel had a miscarriage. Mamma and Ruby went to the base to confront General Wilson about Jewel's tragedy. He said, "I think it was a small price for the young woman to pay for the morale of men willing to lay their lives down for her. It was the least she could do — a small price to pay to keep America free!"

Butterbeans

The worst whipping I ever got was brought on by that Nell Driver, who lived next door.

Miss Nell had the switchboard set up right in the middle of her living room. Every phone call that was made in town had to go through her. Everyone was on a party line, with two or more people sharing the same line. Each party had a code ring to let you know when the call was for you. Our code was three rings and Miss Neta's was two.

More than once, we caught Miss Neta listening in on our conversations. Not a thing went on in town that Nell and Neta didn't know.

Ruby would say, "Those two are the busiest bodies in this heah parish."

If you wanted to know anything that was happening, all you had to do was call Nell and ask, "Do you have a minute?" Of course, she always did and would fill your ear with overexaggerated half-truths.

It had been just a few weeks since Clara was killed, and the little town was still buzzing. All the women in Dixie Roads had sore tongues and swollen jaws from the gossip. The wall phone in the kitchen rang its familiar three rings. Ruby shuffled over and picked up the receiver. So did Miss Neta.

Ruby said into the phone, "Hello, and Miss Neta, honey, I got it."

"Oh, you mean it rang three times? I swear my hearing is getting bad," Miss Neta replied and hung up.

"Big Ruby, is that you?" Nell asked.

"Yes'm," Big Ruby replied.

"Ruby, can you send Cotton over here to play with Linda Gayle and Tom Edward? They are about to drive me crazy. I can't watch them and the switchboard too. It's all lit up like a Christmas tree." She clicked off without waiting for a reply.

Ruby could hear her asking over the static, "Number ple-e-ase."

Nell Driver had two children, Linda Gayle, who was my age, and Tom Edward, Jr., who was only two. Her husband, Tom Edward, Sr., was stationed in France fighting the war from behind a desk. On her meager wages, she tried to raise her two children alone.

She missed not having a man around to take care of her, and Ruby said that most of all she missed their nights in bed together.

Ruby walked to the screen and hollered, "Cotton, go on over to Miss Nell's, and John, you come on in the house."

I left John in the swing and walked across our yard through the hole in the hedge, trying to avoid getting sand burrs in my bare feet. As I climbed the front steps and walked into Nell's living room, Jake was sneaking out the back door. I ran to the door and peered at him through the screen.

No one knew what was going on with Jake and Nell except Big Ruby. She was hiding on the other side of the hedge when Jake ducked down and passed through to our yard.

"I caught ya, ya mannish rascal!" she screeched.

Jake nearly died. Panting, trying to catch his breath, he said, "Gawd dog, Mamma! You almost gave me a stroke."

"Ya wouldn't be so scared if ya wasn't guilty as hell," she replied, turning him around and kicking his butt all the way home. "If ya gets caught with dat white woman, Sheriff Adcock's gonna hang yore smart ass from the nearest oak tree," she warned him.

When I went back to the living room, Nell was sitting in front of the flashing lights on the busy switchboard. She was dressed in a long, flowing flower-print housedress, painting her claw-like fingernails bright red. Her head was bent to one side and she held the receiver in the crook of her neck, babbling away. When she saw me, she returned the little brush to the bottle of polish. Poofing her ratted hair-do, she beckoned with a long red claw.

Between pulling and plugging the wires, she handed me an empty china cup and saucer and asked me if I would go in the kitchen and get her another cup of java. I took the cup as she lit a long Chesterfield cigarette.

In the kitchen, a strong pot of coffee was boiling over on the gas range. I filled the chipped cup with the syrupy black liquid and, spilling a little in the saucer, returned to the buzzing switchboard. Miss Nell took the cup and saucer in one nervous hand and after a few "number pleases" her red glossy lips mouthed, "Thanks, sugar pie."

She gestured to the open door of the bedroom, where I guessed Linda Gayle and Tom Edward must be playing. Entering the room, I found Linda playing dolls on the floor and Tom Edward sitting on the bed, sucking his thumb.

Linda looked up and said, "Oh, Cotton, I'm so glad you came over. Now what do you want to play?"

I thought for a minute and said, "Let's us play war." By then, Tom Edward was fast asleep.

I said, "You be the dirty Jap and I'll shoot you."

I picked up one of Tom Edward's guns and began to chase Linda Gayle around the room. Finally, I penned her in the closet and shot her. After being shot about ten times, she fell out of the closet, staggering and moaning. She made her way to the bed and fell over dead next to the sleeping Tom.

Immediately, I switched the game to a more familiar one, doctor and nurse. I put the gun aside and scratched around in Linda's and Tom's overloaded toy box, looking for Linda's doctor's kit. I found it and quickly donned the white surgery uniform and mask.

"Now young woman, where did he shoot you?" I asked, imitating Doc Parkes.

"I think he shot me, you know, here," she said, pointing under her dress.

We had played these games before. I ran to the door to see what Miss Nell was doing. She was busy as an octopus, arms flying and mouth flapping.

"I'll have to examine you," I said, returning to Linda.

As I pulled her panties down, I took out the little flashlight that came with the doctor's kit and looked between her legs.

"Young woman, you are very sick," I said, reaching into the bag and pulling out a mason jar full of dried butterbeans.

We used the beans for pills. I pushed four or five inside her. Once they were in, I took out a large band-aid and placed it lengthwise over the butterbeans.

"Now, don't take them out or you will surely die," I advised her.

About that time, Nell came to the door.

"Cotton, Big Ruby says it's time for you to come home," she said.

I left Miss Nell and Linda, totally forgetting about the butter-beans.

Shortly after I arrived home, the telephone rang three times. Ruby answered it to find a screaming Nell on the other end.

"Doc Parkes is not in his office and Cotton has put something in Linda Gayle's little pocketbook!" she screamed. "I've got to get her over to the doctor's office in Vivian! It's an emergency! Oh, that horrible child. Ruby, you ought to tear his butt up! Can you send Jewel over to mind the switchboard while I get Linda to the doctor?"

Big Ruby hung up the phone, sent Jewel to Miss Nell's, and made me cut a switch.

Jewel arrived to find Miss Nell trying to get the screaming Linda Gayle and Tom Edward ready for the thirty-minute drive to Vivian. She handed the headpiece and plugs to a bewildered Jewel, telling her to take over. When she began to dress Tom Edward in his short pants, she found his diaper sopping wet.

Cursing, she took off the wet diaper and tied a string around Tom's little penis.

"That should hold him till we get to the doctor," she said to Jewel, who was busy trying to figure out the light board.

Nell grabbed her fake mink coat and the two children and headed out the door to her Model T Ford. As she struggled to get the screaming children into the car, she dropped her hand-bag, which landed in a huge pile of bird-dog shit. Without realizing what had happened, Miss Nell scooped the bag off the ground and mashed it under her arm. She slid under the wheel and raced away toward Vivian.

After a few minutes, she began to smell a shitty odor. Eyes watering, she pulled onto the shoulder of the highway. She spanked poor Tom Edward and checked his diaper. To her surprise, it was clean. She pulled the car back on the road again and continued on her way.

In Vivian, she stopped the car in front of the drugstore. She checked her high heels and the children's shoes, but still could not find where the strong smell was coming from. By this time, she was nauseous and turning green because the odor was so awful.

She brushed her sweaty hair from her eyes and slapped at the flies swarming in the car. Reaching for her handbag so that she could apply some fresh lipstick, she finally discovered the yellow dogshit. It was smeared all over her bag and matted under the arm of her fur coat.

Losing control, she started blowing the car horn. A young boy with a quizzical look on his face sauntered over to the car. Cautiously, he approached the open window to discover a com-pletely mad woman who was slapping flies and kids and smelled like dogshit.

"What can I do for you, Miss?" he asked.

The smell almost knocked him off his feet. He backed away from the car, pinching his nose with his fingers.

"One of my kids has made do-do. Can you please get me some wet towels and a small bottle of Tabu perfume?" she said hysterically, handing him a five-dollar bill. "You can keep the change, sugar, if you will please hurry."

He went into the store and returned with the things she had ordered. As he stepped back on the sidewalk, he watched her smear the dogshit into the fur with the towels and douse herself with perfume. The smell got much worse. Now there was the smell of dogshit, wet fur, and Tabu.

The doctor made stinky Nell and a blue Tom Edward wait in the car. He examined Linda Gayle and found that there was no serious damage done. When he returned her to the smelly car, he told Nell from a distance that Linda would be okay. She was just scared and not hurt.

"Mamma, I got to pee-pee!" cried Tom Edward.

Nell had forgotten about the string. Laying him on the side of the car, she removed his diaper to find his little penis swollen and discolored. She untied the string and he exploded all over her. Now the odor of urine was added to the list!

On the way home, the smell became unbearable in the closed-up car. When Nell reached Dixie Roads, she rolled down the window and threw the coat out. Just as she threw it, she passed Miss Neta in her fine car.

Nosy Neta was on her nightly spin, trying to find something new to gossip about. As she drove slowly down Main Street, her headlights revealed the fur in the middle of the road. She ran over it before coming to a stop.

"My God!" she screamed to herself. "What was that big hairy thing I just hit?" Her car was sitting right on top of the fur coat. She opened the door and saw it sticking out from under the front wheels. "Oh my God! I have run over and killed a bear!" she screeched, driving off in a panic to find the sheriff.

Amy and Dolly, from the Stevens's plantation, were watching as they stood in front of Beason's Grocery.

"Miss Neta has run over something big and hairy in the road," Amy told Dolly.

As Miss Neta pulled away, they walked into the street and made a slow circle around the coat.

"What in tarnation is it?" Dolly asked.

"I don't know, but whatever it is, it is as dead as a doornail and already a-stinkin'," Amy replied.

When Nell got home, she immediately gave Sister Jesse the two full bottles of Tabu that she had gotten for Christmas. Huffily, she related the whole tale.

Needless to say, I wasn't allowed to play with Linda Gayle and Tom Edward anymore. I was given the whipping of my life by Big Ruby, and Tom Edward's little penis was never the same!

Miss Neta Palmer and Sister Go to Town

For about twenty-five years, Miss Neta taught all the aspiring young pianists in Dixie Roads. She did, however, make time for other things, according to Sister Jesse.

Every Wednesday evening, like clockwork, Mamma, Jesse, Nell, and Miss Neta would play bridge for hours. On this particular evening, the talk was mostly about the war.

"Titty your cards, girls. Miss Elsie, have you thought about next year?" asked Miss Neta.

"Why, Miss Neta, what do you mean? With this war, I have been just living from day to day," Mamma replied.

"No, I mean about Cotton Candy," said Miss Neta.

"What about Cotton Candy?" Mamma asked.

"When school starts, Cotton will be ready for first grade," Miss Neta said.

"So, don't beat around the bush," Mamma said.

"Well, the child has no manners, and you can't understand what the poor little thing is saying. He talks just like a pick-aninny," Neta fussed. "And you know, you really should cut his hair. He looks just like a little ole gal."

"Oh, I just couldn't cut that long beautiful hair! It's too pretty!" Mamma cried.

Sister Jesse piped up, saying in her best English, "Well, it certainly isn't any of my doings. It's all Ruby's fault. Gawd knows I'ves tried."

Miss Neta interrupted her by saying, "I've, not I'ves, Sister Jesse."

"Well, that will all be straightened out in school, isn't that true? Well, anyway, the child is my responsibility. Play cards. I believe it's your bid, Nell," Mamma said, ending the discussion.

After the game was over, Miss Neta asked Mamma if she might borrow Sister Jesse the next evening to drive with her over to the Women's Department Club meeting.

"That will be perfectly fine," Mamma said.

After saying good-night, Mamma and Sister Jesse walked across the cool, fragrant yard to the Big House. Nell waited for Mamma and Jesse to go inside, then she made a beeline for Jake, who was waiting in the shadows of a redbud tree.

The next day, Sister Jesse neglected her household duties and spent the whole morning getting ready for the trip to Shreveport. She rolled her reddish hair in rags, starched and ironed her navy dress, and polished her patent leather shoes with vaseline. Then she powdered her brown, freckled skin with rice powder to get it as white as she could.

Amos was next door at Miss Neta's. He had backed the dark silver Rolls-Royce out of the garage into the drive and spit-polished it to a blinding shine. The car was his pride and joy, even though it belonged to Miss Neta.

The Rolls was used for shopping trips to Dallas, meetings in Shreveport, and Miss Neta's nightly spins around Dixie Roads looking for gossip. Once a year in the spring, Amos would put on a chauffeur's uniform and fill the cut-glass vases with roses. He would help Miss Neta into the plush back seat and pull the lace curtain. As she sipped the martini that Amos had poured for her, they would head for "Big D" and the opening of the opera season.

Miss Neta was going to drive the Rolls herself to the meeting. Sister Jesse was allowed to sit in the front seat next to her. They were both dressed up like sore toes.

"They look like two big cows with high heels on," Big Ruby remarked.

Jesse had on her starched, stiff navy dress and a huge flowered hat. Miss Neta wore full-length gloves, a small hat with a veil, and tons of real jewelry from Neiman's. She also carried a purse and an umbrella, just in case it rained. Both ladies smelled as if they had taken a bath in Evening in Paris perfume. Miss Neta was girdled so tightly she could hardly get into the car. Ruby, Jewel, Amos, and I were standing way back in the yard watching their departure.

"Ya'll get way back so you won't get run over," Miss Neta ordered.

Once behind the wheel, she pulled her gloves up and turned around. Jesse did the same. Miss Neta threw her arm over the back of the front seat, blew the veil out of her eyes, and pushed down on the gas pedal. The big silver car jerked forward into the garage while the two women were still turned around.

Amos scooted in after them. He yelled back to us that Sister and Miss Neta were fine and the car didn't have a scratch on her, but the garage was a mess. The bumper of the Rolls had knocked a gaping hole in the back of the garage.

Amos backed the car out of the drive, parked it on the street, put it in first gear, and once again turned it over to Miss Neta. Finally, the women roared off into the lengthening evening shadows with their lights blazing.

After they arrived in Shreveport, Jesse was not allowed to mingle with the white ladies. She was sent to the kitchen with the other colored women to help serve.

Miss Neta delivered her paper on day lilies to the jittery old Victorian ladies who were perpetually afraid that some colored man was going to jump out of the shadows and molest them. They sat fanning themselves with copies of the paper as Miss Neta droned on. Eventually, refreshments were served and the meeting adjourned.

Neta and Jesse packed the car and started back to Dixie Roads. Driving down Texas Street trying to find the way home, Miss Neta made two wrong turns. As she corrected her second mistake there was a loud bump, then a clang and a rattle.

"What in the name of sweet Jesus was that?" Miss Neta cried, sticking her veiled face out of the car window to check the top and make sure there wasn't some colored man up there.

"I think something has fallen off the car," Jesse stated.

Neta wheeled the car over to the curb and came to a stop.

"Jesse, you get out and see what has happened," Miss Neta ordered.

Jesse got out of the car and walked to the back, out of sight in the dark.

"Yep, something has fallen off the car. Something big. Come here, Miss Neta, and help me put it in the trunk. It's too heavy for me to lift by myself," Jesse called from the rear of the car.

Neta pulled the brake, opened the car door, and fell to her knees like a cow in a bog.

"Oh sweet mother of Gawd! I've had a stroke, Jesse! Oh, Jesse, come quick! I'm numb from the waist on down," Neta screamed.

Jesse surveyed Miss Neta piled in the gutter. Knowingly, she reached under Miss Neta's dress and loosened her corset. In a few minutes, the feeling returned to Miss Neta's blood-starved legs.

Neta pulled herself out of the gutter, straightened her dress and hat, then joined Jesse behind the car. Together, they struggled and strained to get a huge metal object into the trunk of the Rolls. Once the metal was loaded, they continued home, sweaty and exhausted.

In an hour or so, they arrived at Miss Neta's. Pulling into the drive, Miss Neta blew the horn for Amos.

"Oh, Amos, come quick. Look, something fell off the car, but we got it," Neta said as she stood beside the opened trunk.

"What? Where?" Amos asked as he stumbled across the yard, half-asleep.

Breathlessly, Miss Neta pointed inside the trunk. Amos shined his flashlight inside to find a manhole cover. Written on it was "Property of Shreveport, Louisiana." Amos was still laughing the next morning when he came to the Big House for breakfast.

Miss Elladee's Strange Baby

One day the mailman delivered a letter for Big Ruby. Ruby hadn't received much mail since Madame X and she was all excited. The whole house was curious about who it was from. She called us all together at the kitchen table to tell us a tale that related to the letter and Miss Elladee Palmer's strange baby.

"Cotton, 'fore you was even thought about and 'fore ya'll came to Dixie Roads . . ." Ruby started saying.

"Big Ruby, you talk all the time. Let me tell it," Jesse said, and this is the story she told us.

★　★　★

Miss Elladee was Miss Neta Palmer's younger sister. Like Miss Neta, she was unmarried and she, too, was a music teacher. She taught singing and the potato flute to grades one through twelve at the country school in Rooster Crossing, Arkansas. School being over for the season, she came to spend the summer with her sister at the family home in Dixie Roads.

Miss Elladee had been courting Oscar Short, a textbook salesman from Texarkana, Arkansas. They had been seeing each other for about a year whenever he was in Rooster Crossing. Within a month of her arrival at Miss Neta's, poor Elladee found she was pregnant. Miss Elladee took the bus to Texarkana to track down Oscar Short, only to find he was already married and had ten kids. She returned to Dixie Roads and told Miss Neta about her predicament, to which her sister said, "You have brought shame on our family's name, and if you are going to have that little bastard, you will have to take a room somewhere else. You cannot stay with me."

Of course, in the forties an unmarried pregnant schoolteacher was not treated with any degree of respect, so Miss Elladee took a room with Mrs. Annie Kellog, who ran a boarding house in downtown Dixie Roads.

Miss Elladee became the butt of many jokes and her nine months were pure hell. She never came out of the boarding house except to go across the street to Doc Parkes's office for routine checkups. Ruby and the colored folks were the only people in town that would have anything to do with her. Big Ruby would go by and check on her every day to see if she was doing all right and if she needed anything.

On one of Ruby's visits, a very peculiar thing happened. Ruby went around the large, white, two-story house and climbed the steps on the side where Miss Elladee had taken a room on the second floor. She knocked on the door, but there was no answer. She put her big ear up against the door, and it came open. She peered inside to find Miss Elladee lying across the bed, buck naked and crying.

Ruby asked, "What in the good Lord is wrong with you, Miss Elladee, sugar?"

Miss Elladee turned over, clutching the bedspread up around her. She whimpered, "Oh, Ruby, I'm so sick!" She pointed to the floor beside the bed.

Ruby turned on the bare light bulb to find that Miss Elladee had turned over the slop jar. Ruby said, "Now, sugar, stop all that whining. Big Ruby will clean it up. Now jest pull yourself together and lay back and relax." She got a mop out of the closet and began to scrub. When she had everything cleaned up, she sat on the side of the bed and rubbed Miss Elladee's feet. Ruby asked, "Did you have anything to eat, honey?"

Miss Elladee shook her head no. She told Ruby that she had been so sick all morning that she couldn't eat a bite. But if Ruby didn't mind, she would love a big lemon Coke from the cafe. Ruby said she didn't mind. Miss Elladee reached for her handbag and gave Ruby a quarter. She told Ruby to get herself one, too.

Quarter and mop in hand, Ruby started down the long stairs, passing the window where all the boarders were having dinner with Mrs. Kellog. Ruby peeked in to find six people sitting around the massive table. Miss Annie was at one end, passing the fried chicken gravy.

She said, "Hank, take this gravy, something wet has dripped on my head." Looking up, she saw a wet bulge in the wallpapered ceiling. Then she noticed Ruby at the open window and hollered, "Hey gal, would you bring that mop in here? Something is dripping from the ceiling."

Ruby went around the house to the back door and came into the dining room.

Annie told her, "Now, honey, take that mop handle and poke at that bulge in the wallpaper."

Ruby poked at the bulge, and the wallpaper split, and something plopped into the peas, splashing all over the boarders. Ruby just backed out of the door as everyone, smelling their hands and the table, figured out what it was. Ruby got the lemon Cokes and started back up to Miss Elladee's room. Passing the window again, she heard Miss Annie saying, "Yes, Hank, it's shit. I know shit when I smell it. It's all in the peas."

Ruby grabbed her bosom and started laughing. She literally rolled into Miss Elladee's room, screaming with laughter.

Miss Elladee asked, "What in the world are you laughing at, Big Ruby?"

Ruby couldn't stop laughing long enough to tell her the tale, and in a few minutes they were both in hysterics. When Ruby finally got the story out, they laughed most of the afternoon. As she left, Ruby said to Miss Elladee, "It serves um right for all the mean things they have said about you, sugar!"

Then she turned to Miss Elladee and whispered, "Eat shit and die!" With that, they both just hollered.

When the time came for Miss Elladee to have the baby, she packed her little suitcase and went across the street to Doc

Parkes's office. She took a seat in the waiting room and waited and waited for Doc Parkes. He never did show up. Later we found out he was out in the country delivering a mule.

As coincidence would have it, crazy Bernice Harkness, the Harkness boys' mamma, was Doc Parkes's receptionist. She was nervous as a cat by nature, and when the doctor didn't show up all afternoon, she took a shot of whiskey and called Miss Neta. Bernice told Miss Neta that Miss Elladee was in serious trouble, to which Miss Neta responded, "Yes, I know."

Hysterical, Bernice shouted, "Someone needs to get her to Shreveport real quick before she has the thing right here on the waitin' room floor!"

The news had to go through the switchboard at Nell Driver's. As usual, it was all over town in no time at all. Big Ruby ran next door to talk some sense into Miss Neta and found her sitting at the table, staring off into space and talking to herself.

She was saying, "How could she do this to me? Get me involved in this scandalous mess." The phone rang two times, bringing Miss Neta out of her trancelike state. She turned to Big Ruby and said, "Can you please get that? I'm so weak in the knees I can't get up."

Ruby answered the phone to find a panicked Bernice on the other end of the line. "Someone, please, come quick," Bernice said. "I don't know a thing about catchin' babies. Miss Elladee is in a lot of pain. What should I do? I think she has broken her water. Forget taking her to Shreveport, it's too late. Help! Please, help!" And she hung up.

Ruby dropped the receiver and ran into the backyard, screaming for Amos and Jake, who were in the flower beds. She hollered through the back door of the Big House for Jewel to come quick. She turned to Amos and young Jake and told them to hitch up the mule wagon and meet them at Doc Parkes's — and to hurry.

Jewel and Big Ruby ran out of the yard and headed to Doc Parkes's office, where they found that Bernice had moved Miss Elladee into the clinic. She had her lying on her back on a stretcher, covered with a sheet. Miss Elladee had her knees up and spread open. Bernice had a flashlight, looking under the sheet.

Ruby said to Bernice, "What do you see under there?"

Bernice said, "Oh, thank Gawd ya'll are here! I think I can see the head." Ruby took the flashlight from Bernice's trembling hand and looked for herself. She said, "Nah, that jest some hair round Miss Elladee's pocketbook."

About that time, Amos came shuffling into the clinic. He said, "Big Ruby, I's done what you said. Jake gots the mule wagon out front."

Ruby said, "Now, ya'll are goin' to have to help me git Miss Elladee out to the wagon. Now hurry up!"

They all pushed the stretcher out the front door and over to the mule and wagon. Miss Elladee screamed.

Jewel said, "It's all right, sugar. We's tryin' to be gentle. It will all be over soon."

Amos and Jake lifted the big pregnant woman off the stretcher and onto the wagon. Bernice Harkness rushed back into the office, screaming that she was going to try and get the doctor. Jake got into the wagon with Miss Elladee and turned the mule up the main street with Ruby, Amos, and Jewel running behind in the dust.

They pulled up to Ruby's front porch, unloaded Miss Elladee and rushed her inside to Ruby's bed. Ruby took over. She told Jewel to boil lots of water. She and Amos got Miss Elladee ready. The two of them had done this many times before, as most of the colored women had their babies at home.

Jewel sat on the side of the bed and tried to console the poor, swollen woman. She wiped her forehead with a cool cloth and said, "Hush, honey, what kind of baby you wants?"

Delirious and in obvious pain, Miss Elladee answered, "A boy, a girl, a boy-girl — ooh, it don't matter!"

In a while, there was a big push and a scream. Ruby held up the squalling baby and handed it to Amos. Then she went back to tending to Miss Elladee. Amos took the baby over to a little hand tub that had been prepared with an herb solution and began bathing the child. Suddenly he stepped back in disbelief and said, "Well, would ya look at dis heah? Ruby, Jewel, come quick and look at dis!" They both came over and looked into the bathwater.

"Miss Elladee sho' got her wish. She got a boy-girl!" Amos said.

"Mamma, what is it?" asked Jewel.

"Well, I'll be dawged!" Ruby whispered. Reaching between the squirming baby's legs, she said, "Look, dis child has a boy's thang and a girl's thang! I's heard about such, but I's never seen one up close."

Jewel was completely confused by now and said, "What you call something like that?"

Ruby scratched her head and said, "I thinks you call it a morfidite."

Miss Elladee was sound asleep. Jewel whispered to her mamma, "What's we gonna tell her when she wakes up?"

"I don't rightly know," Ruby said. "She'll prob'ly sleep all night. Poor thang is all tuckered out."

They tiptoed out of the little house to let Miss Elladee get her much-needed rest. Ruby and Jewel went over to Miss Neta's to break the news to her. They walked into her kitchen to find Miss Neta in the same place at the table, staring off into space.

Ruby broke the silence by saying, "Miss Neta, Miss Elladee had a healthy baby."

Miss Neta looked up and said, "Well, what is the little bastard?"

Ruby and Jewel looked at each other for a minute, then Ruby said, "Well, ma'am, we can't rightly tell."

Miss Neta said, "What do you mean you can't tell?" She stood up and pushed her chair back, looking at the two for an explanation.

Ruby said, "Well, it's got dis heah gal's thang and it got dis heah boy's thang, too."

Neta's back straightened as she said, "Are you trying to tell me the child has two *thangs*?"

"Yes'm," Jewel said.

With that, Miss Neta bolted straight up and fell across the kitchen table in a dead faint.

The next day, Miss Nell had the news all over town before Miss Elladee herself knew. Miss Elladee's strange baby had the town buzzing.

Ruby and Jewel tiptoed into the little house and woke Miss Elladee for her to see her new child. They placed the small bundle, wrapped in a blanket, next to its groggy mother. Her eyes opened and Miss Elladee started talking to the little baby and caressing it.

Ruby said to her, "Me, Jewel, and Amos is gonna go out onto the porch so you and yo' baby can get acquainted. If ya'll need anythin', we be right heah."

They stepped outside, leaving the new mamma with her baby. In a few minutes a blood-curdling scream came from inside the house. They ran back in to find an ashen Miss Elladee up on her knees in the middle of the bed, pointing between the child's legs and screaming, "It's a freak! Get it away from me! Do ya hear! Get this *thing* away!"

Ruby reached down to pick up the wiggling baby. That baby latched onto Miss Elladee's long hair and hung on for dear life. Miss Elladee and the baby were eye to eye and the baby broke into a big grin. Miss Elladee collapsed on the bed next to the contented child and began to cry, hugging the small creature to her bosom.

Ruby turned to Jewel and Amos and said, "Let's us git out of heah. Everythin' will be all right now. Nature will take its course."

They left the two alone all afternoon. Later, Jewel went in to see how they were doing. She found Miss Elladee rocking her new baby in Ruby's rocker and nursing it.

Jewel asked quietly, "What's ya gonna name it?"

After a minute, Miss Elladee winked and said, "I think I will call it Jimmie Sue." They both laughed, shaking their heads.

People came from all over the place to try and get a look at the little creature, but Miss Elladee was very protective of the baby. No one got to see it.

Months passed, and one day a man came to the house from the "Show of Shows Circus" to talk to Miss Elladee. She let him in, and they talked most of the afternoon. The next day the man came back again for Miss Elladee and Jimmie Sue. Miss Elladee called Ruby, Amos, and Jewel up on the front porch.

With her suitcases and Jimmie Sue in hand, she said, "This nice man is gonna provide a place for Jimmie Sue and me. He isn't gonna let anything harm us. He says we can travel with his circus until Jimmie Sue gets a bit older and then he will find the child a place with the show."

She told Ruby how much she appreciated all of them for their help and concern in her time of need. She had done nothing but think for the last few months and she was sure she had made the right decision for the both of them. Miss Elladee took up her suitcases and Jimmie Sue, got in the man's big car, and they left Dixie Roads forever.

★　★　★

After Jesse finished her story, Ruby began reading the letter: "Dear Ruby and all, Jimmie Sue and I are fine. We have traveled all over the United States with the circus. He's almost grown and we have been treated well. Jimmie Sue is performing as the Bearded Lady. Tell Miss Neta that I forgive her. Love, Miss Elladee Palmer."

Ruby wiped a tear out of her eye and said, "Now there is a smart woman for ya."

Opal Jean's

Indian summer crept upon us as quietly as an Indian walking on leaves. The long hot days were giving way to shorter days and cooler nights. The fruit harvest was abundant and ready to pick. Earlier in the summer, there had been gallons of plums and figs. Now there were bushels of pears, apples, and grapes—all to be transformed into jellies, preserves, relishes, and juices. Soon, it would be time for Amos to make his famous wine from the wild possum grapes and muscadines.

Most of the summer flowers and greenery had given way to the hot dry weather, leaving everything a dusty brown. One of the first signs that fall was on its way was the Indian paintbrush, glowing bright red and orange. It filled the corners of the yard and bordered the ditches beside the road.

The cooler mornings elicited a quicker step from the women in the kitchen. The mail had come earlier than usual, and Ruby had received yet another letter. This one was from Opal Jean, Ruby's older sister, who lived in the woods of Arkansas. Opal wrote once a year, always in the fall. Ruby called us to the kitchen table to read the long-awaited letter, which contained a year's worth of news.

Ruby began, "Dear Ruby and family, My husband, Clyde, and me be fine, as well as our children. Lessie be almost grown now and last week Teddy and Freddy, my twin boys, turned five years, same age as yore John. The summer this year was powerfully hot. It took its toll on us and wood ticks like to have carried us off.

But, praise Jesus, it is gettin' cooler now and the life is comin' back in all of us. I feel like we can make it now. I shore wish somehow ya'll could come up to see us. It be so long since I set eyes on you and yore children, Jake and Jewel. They was just babies and I ain't never seen John and Girthalene. I pray I get to see ya'll soon, we's got a lot of catchin' up to do. Yore lovin' sister, Opal Jean."

As Ruby finished the letter, she bowed her head and began to cry. Near the end of the letter, Mamma had come into the kitchen for a drink of water.

Turning from the sink, Mamma said, "Now, now, Ruby don't cry. Just how long has it been since you have seen your sister?"

Ruby rubbed her wet eyes with her apron and replied thoughtfully, "It be almost twelve years, now," and she continued to bawl.

Mamma said, "Well, that's too long. Now you straighten yourself up." She paused, then said, "It's about time for you to go a-visiting."

Ruby looked up from the crumpled letter and was about to say something when Mamma continued, "We can do without ya'll for a few days. Can't we, Sister? My husband and I will go to the train depot tomorrow and purchase three tickets for Jewel, Jake, and you to go to Arkansas." She paused again, then said, "John, Girthalene, and Cotton won't need tickets because they are just babies."

For a few seconds, we were struck dumb. When Mamma's words finally hit us, we joined each other in the middle of the kitchen and danced around in a circle like a bunch of "wild banshees" (to quote one of Sister Jesse's favorite expressions).

John and I looked at each other with wide eyes and said at the same time, "A train ride, a real train ride to Arkansas!"

The next few days were busy ones. We helped Big Ruby with her chores—washing, starching, and ironing our clothes, then packing them in three large suitcases. We were so excited that the time flew by.

The morning of the train trip, we were all up before dawn. By four-thirty that morning, Big Ruby and Jewel had baked homemade rolls, fried a large chicken, and placed it all in a large hatbox along with apples, pears, and grapes for us to eat along the way.

Daddy walked into the kitchen and said, "Everything has been taken care of. Opal Jean and Clyde have been notified as to your arrival."

He handed Ruby an envelope that contained our tickets and instructions on how we were to get to our destination. Once more, Daddy sat at the table with Ruby and carefully went over the plans.

"When you get to Texarkana you have to get off the train and wait in the depot for two hours before you catch the train to Hope, Arkansas. When you get on the train to Hope, you must tell the conductor that you are the party that wants to get off at a place called Nine Forks. It's about twelve miles just this side of Hope," he finished.

The sun was just peeking over the horizon, casting pink shadows on the clouds, as we pulled up to the little yellow depot. Ruby told John, Girthalene, and me to stop fidgeting. Of course, we could not sit still. We were so excited!

As we left the car, a huge black and silver train chugged slowly up the tracks into the station, blowing off steam as it came to a screeching halt before us. The conductor jumped off the train and announced, "All aboard for Texarkana!"

My daddy turned and said, "That's your train."

We hugged Mamma and Daddy, saying our good-byes. Daddy handed the conductor our baggage and helped us onto the train.

He told Big Ruby, "You take care of Cotton, ya hear? The child has never been away from home. Miss Elsie and I think traveling will be educational for him."

"Don't worry yoreself none," Ruby replied.

When we were on the train, the conductor looked us over and said, "You colored folks will have to find seats at the back of the car. The white child can sit wherever he wants to."

"The white chile is with us and we will all set together," Ruby huffily told the conductor.

She found two seats in the back. Jake placed our baggage over the seats as Jewel pushed Girthalene, John, and me into the seat in front of the others. We pressed our faces into the window to wave at Mamma and Daddy. The train jerked forward.

"It's movin'!" screamed John.

The train picked up speed, and in no time at all we had lost sight of Mamma, Daddy, and Dixie Roads. Once we were on our way, John and I left the seat to explore the massive train. We saw a fat white lady with a small red-haired girl. We watched her as she held the child up to drink from a water cooler. John tried to drink from the same cooler.

The fat woman said meanly, "I guess you have never been on a train before, boy, but niggers are not allowed to drink after white folks. You have your own cooler over there marked 'colored.' And, I might add, you also have your own restroom marked plainly." Then the woman grabbed my arm tightly.

"Where's your mamma? Does she know you are playing with this here little nigger?" she hissed at me.

I pulled away from her, pointing to Big Ruby.

"That's my mammy and he is my brother John," I sassed. Imitating Jake, I said, "And you can kiss my white butt!"

The woman put her hand over her large red mouth to muffle a cry. She grabbed the little girl, jerking a knot in her neck, and headed back to their seat in the front of the car. After she was seated, the woman began whispering to the other white folks and pointing to us. By now, everyone in the car was staring in our direction.

"John, you and Cotton sit down. Now, what have ya'll been doing to make everyone stare at us that-a-way?" Ruby asked.

"I heard Cotton tell that ole white lady to kiss his white butt," Jake said, trying to hide his toothy grin.

Ruby grabbed the hatbox and shoved some fruit at us. Still snickering, we settled back in our seats to watch the ever-changing scenery whiz by the window.

An hour later, the train started slowing down. From the window, we could see the town of Texarkana. It was the largest town this side of Shreveport.

The conductor stood between the cars and bellowed, "Next stop TEX-AR-KANA!"

We gathered our belongings as the train came to a teeth-jarring halt. Ruby lost her footing and fell against the lady with the red-haired child, knocking them to the floor. Jake tried to help the lady and child up, but the woman pushed him away. She grabbed the child by the hand and got off the train.

We heard her mumble, "What is the world coming to? How is it possible for a colored woman to have a child as white as cotton? I'll just declare!"

Jewel was laughing hysterically. "Mamma, you really knocked the hot air out'n dat white lady!" she squealed.

"Hush up! Get hold of John. Jake, you carry Girthalene. Cotton, you grab a hold of my dress tail and hang on real tight. Ya'll don't forget nothin'. Now move!" Big Ruby ordered.

We found the colored section of the depot and spread all of our belongings out on a long wooden bench. Girthalene fell asleep in Ruby's lap while Ruby read a copy of *True Romance* she was carrying in her pocket. Jewel found a discarded newspaper and looked at the pictures.

"Let's go for a walk and look around," Jake suggested to John and me. We went outside and walked along the platform, watching the busy station as trains pulled in and out.

After a while, we got bored and went back inside the depot.

"I's looked everywhere and I can't find a bathroom for colored folks and I's got to go in a bad way," we heard Jewel tell Ruby.

About that time, another train came into the station, and the colored section of the depot emptied as everyone else boarded the train. Looking around, Ruby said, "There ain't no one around, go in that closet. I looked in a while ago and there is a coal bucket in there. Use it."

Jewel walked into the closet, closing the door. In a few minutes, she reappeared, looking relieved.

The train to Hope came rumbling up the tracks. Once again, Ruby got everything together and pushed us toward the waiting train. As we left the depot, she glanced back to make certain we hadn't left any of our belongings. She saw a dark yellow stream running under the closet door, making a puddle on the dirty floor.

"I guess that ole coal bucket had a hole in it," she remarked.

Laughing as we boarded the train, we looked for seats in the back and sat down. Girthalene was wiggling in Ruby's lap when Jewel noticed that one of Girthalene's little sandals was missing.

"Mamma, don't look now, but Girthalene has lost one of her shoes," Jewel said.

We all looked for the missing shoe under seats and up and down the aisles, but to no avail.

"What's we gonna do, Mamma? We can't go a-visitin' with little sister in one shoe," Jewel said.

Ruby thought for a minute, then said, "I'll fix it. Don't ya'll worry none." She reached up and got a suitcase. Rummaging through it, she found a dingy white slip. She tore off the hem and bandaged Girthalene's foot.

"If anyone ask ya, Girthalene hurt her foot," Ruby said with a wink.

John and I took Girthalene up and down the aisles, teaching her how to limp on the bandaged foot.

When the conductor came by for the tickets, Ruby told him that we were the party that wanted off at Nine Forks. Jewel opened the hatbox and gave each of us a piece of cold chicken and a roll. We ate as we gazed out the window. The train had left the flat Delta country and was passing through the hilly pine forests of Arkansas and over bridges that spanned cypress swamps. Moss hanging from the misty trees gave the swamps an eerie appearance. The deep, dark forest, with flecks of red and orange from the sumac trees, almost blocked out the sun at times.

At dusk, the conductor came over to Ruby and said, "Ya'll get your belongings together. The next stop will be Nine Forks."

We gathered our belongings and waited between the cars as the train came to a slow stop. The conductor jumped off, released the steps, and helped us to the ground. The train started to move away slowly as he jumped back on.

"In five days, come to this very spot and flag the train down so you can get back home. Now don't forget," he called, waving good-bye. The train huffed and puffed around a pine thicket, moving out of sight in a puff of smoke.

About twenty feet down the tracks was a wagon and two mules. On the wagon sat Opal Jean, Clyde, and Lessie. Opal jumped from the wagon and ran toward us, waving a hand-kerchief.

"Ruby, my baby sister! Is that really you?" she cried.

Compared to Ruby, Opal was skin and bones. They didn't look anything alike. Opal threw her arms around Big Ruby and they both started to cry. In a few minutes, Opal released Ruby to turn to the rest of us.

"Dis heah must be Jewel. My, how pretty you has got to be, all growed up," she said. She gave Jewel a big hug. "My, my, Jake, what a good-lookin' man you turned out to be. And this is little John," she went on as she patted John on his head. She reached down and picked up Girthalene, hugging her close. "Why you are the spittin' image of yo' mamma. Why, Ruby, what happened to Girthalene's foot?" Opal asked full of concern.

"Oh, she hurt it playin' at home. Stuck a rusty nail through it," Ruby lied. She quickly shot us a look filled with warning.

Opal turned to me and said, "And who, may I ask, is this white chile?"

"Dis heah is Cotton. He belongs to the people we work fo' and I guess he's mine, too," Ruby answered.

The women laughed.

"Fo' a minute, Ruby gal, I thought you had taken up with a white man!" Opal exclaimed.

Opal took us to the wagon. Everyone said hi-do to Clyde and Lessie, Opal's husband and daughter. Clyde threw our baggage into the back of the wagon and helped everyone on. Then he headed the two mules into the dark, cool, pine-scented woods as the orange sun began to set.

By the time we reached their log house, the sun had gone down and fireflies were thick as thieves. Two identical little boys were playing on the front porch. They had an old hound dog between them. The dog and the boys bounded off the porch to greet us.

"This must be Freddy and Teddy," Ruby said.

"That it be. You boys come and see yo' Auntie Ruby and yo' cousins, Jake, Jewel, John, Girthalene, and, yes, Cotton too," Opal called.

The boys crowded around me, peering at me with big eyes.

"Mamma, dis chile be as *white* as cotton," Freddy said.

"That's fo' sho'," laughed Opal.

We entered the neat little log house as the inquisitive twins continued looking me up one side and down the other. When we finished putting our things away, we sat down to a supper of fresh eggs, biscuits, homemade sausage, and syrup from their own sugar mill.

Licking his lips, Jake said, "Dis be the best syrup I ever put to my mouth."

Clyde promised to show us how it was made in the morning. After supper, Lessie and Jewel cleared the table while the rest of us sat on the front porch. The twins showed us how Boomer, the hound dog, could fetch, while the grown folks talked of days gone by. Opal rocked Girthalene to sleep, and before long the thrilling day had caught up with John and me. We fell soundly asleep as we lay on the cool floor of the porch.

The next morning, I awoke to find we had all been put together in a single feather bed. Opal appeared in the doorway.

"Everybody rise and shine!" she called. What a sight we must have made, John, the twins, Boomer, and me as we peeked from under the patchwork quilt. "Ya'll look like a nest of possums, three black and one white 'un," Opal laughed.

We were told to go out back to the privy and to wash our hands and neck in the tub under the pump with homemade lye soap. We sat down to a breakfast of buckwheat pancakes with sloe jelly and bacon. We children had large tin cups full of fresh goat's milk, and the older folks had strong-smelling coffee.

After breakfast, Ruby put Girthalene in the dirt by the steps to play. John and I followed Teddy and Freddy around as they did their morning chores. Even in the daylight it was hard to tell them apart. Not only did they look alike, they also talked alike.

The twins took a bucket of oats into the barn and fed and watered their mules, Pete and Repeat. Next came the rabbits, pigs, and chickens. They let John and me gather the eggs, since we did that at home. When we finished with the chickens, the twins tended the goats. Freddy fed them, one at a time, while Teddy milked them. Carrying the bucket of milk to the house, we ran into Clyde, Jake, Jewel, and Lessie on their way to the cane patch. They were going to cut sugarcane and show Jake and Jewel how to make the syrup at the mill.

Clyde told us, "Yo' mamma and her sister have a lot of catchin' up to do so ya'll take the milk in and don't bother them. Then you boys take John and Cotton down to the creek and show um yo' swimmin' hole. You can ride Repeat and don't be gone too long."

We left the milk just inside the back door and ran to get Repeat. All four of us jumped on the mule's wide back and headed for the creek. The early morning had been chilly, but now it was hotter than blue blazes.

We came across a clear, spring-fed creek nestled in the rocky hillside. We jumped down, tied Repeat to a persimmon tree laden with ripening fruit, and raced to the water's edge. The twins took off all their clothes and hung them on a huckleberry bush. They ran to the top of a small cliff and untied a muscadine vine. Both boys grabbed the vine and swung out over the creek, letting go at the same moment to fall into the icy water below.

John looked at me and said, "Gawd dog! Did you see that?"

I said, "Yeah. Come on, let's us try that."

We stripped and followed the twins into the cold water. We splashed and played until we were almost frozen before climbing out onto a bed of soft green moss to rest among the ferns and purple wild violets.

I turned to John and said, "This is the life. They sho' know how to live up here in Arkansas."

Warmed by the hot sun, we dressed and got back on the mule. We plodded home, picking possum grapes all along the way.

They hung all around our heads in the trees. From the mule's back, we could stretch up and grab handfuls of the purple clusters. We found that they weren't very good to eat, but made lip-smacking jelly and wine.

When we reached the house, we unloaded the grapes in the kitchen, then went back outside to find Jake leading Pete around and around in a circle at the sugar mill. As the mill turned, it crushed the sugarcane into thick juice, which was used to make the sugar and syrup. As we watched the mill, we heard a gunshot from the woods. In less than a minute, another shot echoed across the yard. In a short while, Clyde emerged from the woods, dragging a razorback hog by its ears.

John asked, "What did ya kill that big ole pig fo', Uncle Clyde?"

Clyde answered, "It's fo' the pig roast and party we's givin' in yo' honor tonight. Now, ya'll get on back to the house and see what ya'll can do to help. Tell Lessie to come on down here and help me skin this pig."

When we got to the kitchen door, the smells of baking bread and cake almost knocked us over. We entered the hot kitchen, and the twins told Lessie what her father had said. Lessie went out the back door, leaving the cooking for the party to Opal, Ruby, and Jewel.

Just before dusk, Opal Jean announced, "Everything is ready!"

Ruby said, "You little 'uns come with me."

She took us to the bedroom, dressed us all in clean overalls, and sent us to the front porch. "Now, don't youse be gettin' dirty or I'll skin ya'll alive!" she warned.

Leaving us on the porch, the ladies started getting ready. After lots of laughing and squealing, they appeared on the porch in brightly colored, frilly summer dresses with their hair piled high on their heads, held in place with ivory combs. Girthalene had on the tiny starched pinafore that she had worn in the parade back in Dixie Roads.

Jake and Clyde sauntered from around the side of the house wearing plaid shirts and new blue jeans. Their hair glistened from a washing in the creek and rubbed-in vaseline.

"My, my! Don't we all looks pretty?" Opal said. Everyone laughed.

The pig was hanging on a spit over a fire in the yard. Every time someone passed it, they would give it a turn. The kitchen table had been pulled out into the backyard and was brimming over with food. The women had prepared cakes, pies, potato salad, loaves of hot bread, baked beans, and fall greens fresh from the garden. Opal had boiled and fried the pig's innards into chitlins, the grown folks' favorite.

Sam the Fiddler was the first guest to arrive, by foot out of the woods. He came strutting across the yard like a banty rooster. Tipping his hat to Big Ruby, he introduced himself and began playing his squeaky fiddle. Wagon loads of people pulled into the yard. By and by, the party was under way.

Sam the Fiddler jumped on the porch and tore into a hoedown. Everyone went crazy. The men grabbed partners as they danced in a large circle, kicking up dust. John and I grabbed each other, imitating the grown folks, and began to twirl around. We were all under the fiddler's spell, which was enhanced by the smell of the cool, crisp piney woods. Tired and thirsty from all the dancing, we ate our weight in the delicious food.

Ruby finally said, "It's time for you little folks to go to bed, so us older folks can git down to some serious partyin'."

She marched us into the house against our shouts of protest and pleas to stay up just a little longer, tucked us in, and left us in the dark. When she walked outside, the fiddler broke into "Sweet Georgia Brown."

The men opened another bottle of muscadine wine and passed it around. From our bed, we could hear the music, loud laughter, and talking.

Ruby turned to Opal and said, "Girl, I's don't guess I's ever had so much fun. You country folks really know how to throw a hoedown. All this dancin' and drinkin' has made me gotta pee somethin' terrible."

Opal turned to a handful of women and said, "Ruby and me are goin' to visit Auntie Carrie. Ya'll want to come?"

The women walked into the far corner of the backyard in the moonlight, leaving the men on the porch. Some of the older women just kept walking and talking and began to pee standing up. They lifted the hem of their skirts, took a stance, and let go. Ruby and her sister were squatting side by side, peeing in the moonlit backyard behind a small sassafras. Ruby very quietly watched the strange sight as the women cavorted and peed standing up, never missing a step.

She asked Opal, "Did ya see dat, girl? I would have peed all over my legs."

Opal said, "Dat way of life be passed down from the cotton-pickin' days when every minute counted. A colored woman would git forty lashes with a whip if she tarried a second too long. So they's learnt to do everythin' on their feet, even peein'."

Ruby said, "I never."

Opal added, "Most of the women had their babies alongside a cotton row. They left only long enough to take the baby home and clean up and be back to the cotton patch 'fore the sun went down to pick that gawd-damn cotton."

Back in the house, in the dark, the twins said, "Come on. They's should all be's drunk on the wine by now, and we can sneak round and watch um and they'll never know we's sneakin' and watchin'."

We left the bed wearing our longjohns. Barefoot, we tiptoed through the kitchen, onto the back porch, and out into the moonlit backyard. Peeking around the house, we could see Opal Jean and Clyde rocking on the front porch. Big Ruby and Elton Lee Jones, who had been smitten with Ruby on first glance, were drinking wine under a large chinquapin tree and talking in drunken whispers.

"Quick! Hide! Somebody's a-comin'!" John whispered.

We ducked under the house in the cool dirt to see Jake and Lessie walk by hand in hand. Giggling, they moved toward the dark barn and disappeared into it. Everything got really quiet.

An owl hooted in the woods. Freddy asked, "What ya'll think they's be doin' in the barn?"

Teddy said, "Let's us sneak over to the window and see."

We tiptoed, single file, across the backyard to the barn, unnoticed by the other guests, who by now had paired off. Some were passed out all over the yard. We pulled ourselves up to the windowsill and peered into the barn.

When our eyes had adjusted to the light, we saw Jake and Lessie in a pile of straw, the moonlight bathing their naked bodies. Jake rolled over on top of Lessie, and they both began to moan.

"What they be doin'? You think they's fightin'?" the twins whispered.

I said, "Nah, they's jest wrestlin' like Jake and Vera did in the boxcar."

John said, "Well, I hope they's don't have no coon dog puppies."

We moved away from the window to find that everyone was wrestling. We watched for a while, then we went back to bed with wildly beating hearts. As we lay there, we wondered what we would ever do with all those puppies.

The day after the pig roast was Sunday. We got up early and went into the kitchen. There we found all the grown-ups slumped around the table, drinking coffee and hot sassafras tea with honey, nursing their swollen heads.

Jewel fed us, then took us into the bedroom and dressed us in our Sunday clothes.

"Ya'll go out on the porch and don't git dirty before church. We all will be dressed in a little while and ready to go," Jewel told us.

We wore white, heavily starched suits and ties, and our black shoes were spit-shined so glossy that we could see ourselves in them. Eventually, everyone found their way to the front porch, all dressed in their Sunday best. The ladies wore large hats.

Clyde pulled the mule-drawn wagon up to the porch. We piled in and took off into the frosty woods. Shortly, we came to a clearing, and there stood a small white church with a wooden steeple. The churchyard was filled with wagons and a few cars.

When we came to a stop, Jake helped Lessie off the wagon. Elton Lee and his younger brother, Junior, came swaggering over to help Ruby and Jewel down. The rest of us jumped down into the wet grass. By now, the sun had melted the early morning frost.

John and I put Girthalene between us as we marched into the little Southern Baptist church. The preacher stood in the doorway, shaking hands with the congregation. He shook my hand, and said, "Welcome to Mount Olive Baptist Church, chile."

We were sent to Sunday school class, where we sat in a small circle in little handmade chairs. We listened to Miss Margie Jo, the pretty teacher, tell us about Peter and Paul. She taught us how to make a church with our hands folded.

"Here's the church and here's the steeple. Open the door and here are da peoples!" she said.

After Sunday school, we went to the main church for a sermon of hellfire and brimstone. The twins, John, Jewel, Clyde, Elton Lee, Junior, and I sat in the first pew while Jake, Lessie, Opal Jean, and Ruby joined the choir behind the preacher. After an hour and a half of singing, preaching, and the earth's opening up and exposing hell, we filed out of the church onto the grounds.

The hot fires of hell were still smoldering on our faces when we stepped out into the chilly air. A light smoke appeared all around us haloed by the sun. Tables filled with steaming food were placed everywhere for our "dinner on the ground."

One beautiful, cool day flowered into another as our visit wore on. The five days flew by too quickly. I had fallen in love with the Arkansas woods and Opal Jean's family. Before we knew it, it was our last day with Opal, Clyde, Lessie, and the twins. I could tell Jake and Lessie were going to find it hard to say good-bye.

Finally, we gathered together for our last meal. We were to catch the train back to Dixie Roads that evening. The table was set with Opal's best dishes. In the middle of the table was a large platter.

Ruby said, "Uh, umm-um," smacking her lips. "Where did ya'll get those delicious-lookin' squirrels?"

The steaming platter contained a huge mound of rice, on top of which were small, brown, cooked bodies.

Opal turned to Ruby, filling her own plate with the steaming food, and said, "Oh, these ain't squirrels, honey. These be big ole wood rats."

Ruby dropped her spoon, pushed herself away from the table, and said, "I jest lost my appetite." She turned to all of us, looking a little blue around the gills, and said, "Ya'll get yo' things together. We have a long trip ahead of us, and that train gonna be heah soon. Now come on, move."

After teary good-byes, we walked down the dirt road that led to the railroad tracks. Poor Lessie and the twins followed us. Ruby flagged the train down as we said good-bye to each other with hugs and promises. Once again, we boarded the train and headed back to Dixie Roads.

Jake looked at Ruby and asked, "Mamma, what got into you back there at Opal's?"

Ruby replied, "I's jest couldn't stay another second in a house where people eats rats! I don't care if Opal is my sister. 'Sides, you ought to be ashamed of yoreself for carryin' on with yo' own kin!"

I'm sure none of us ever forgot that beautiful Indian summer in the woods of Arkansas at Opal Jean's. Like Daddy said, it was really educational for me. Poor Girthalene had got used to being a cripple, and it took Ruby nearly a month to stop her from limping and complaining.

Turning into a Boy!

We moved on a frosty November morning. My daddy had had some bad luck with the Pig's Foot cafes. Less than a month after our trip to Opal Jean's in Arkansas, the cafe in Ida burned to the ground. The Pig's Foot 2 cafe in Gilliam was robbed. The robbers took everything, stripping the place naked. They even took the jukebox with the colored lights. The Pig's Foot in Dixie Roads wasn't doing well at all because of the new drive-in cafe, the Dairy Sue. The Dairy Sue even had two carhops, girls dressed in dairymaid costumes.

My father always felt a bit guilty about the rejection he had gotten from the military because of his blind eye, so he took a job at an ammunitions plant on the other side of Shreveport. He was hired on as a foreman of the train shops at the big military operation, as he put it, "to help his country in the war effort."

Because I was so young, the idea of leaving my colored friends and Dixie Roads hadn't quite sunk in until Mamma called Ruby and everybody together to break the news.

I sat beside Mamma in the kitchen as she said, "I hate to tell ya'll this, but Mr. William, Cotton, and I will be moving away from Dixie Roads and the Big House. Ya'll are free to go, or you may stay on and work for the Smiths, the new owners of the Big House."

Everyone except Jake was going to stay. He had decided to join the army. When he went down to the post office to sign up, the

124

sergeant in charge sent him home to ask Big Ruby what his last name was.

Jake walked quietly up to the kitchen door and told Big Ruby what the man had said. "Mamma, they's wants to know what my last name is before I can join the army."

Ruby backed softly from the sink full of dirty dishes and walked very slowly over to the door where her son was. Her brow furrowed with worry. Jesse, who was sitting at the table, all of a sudden was all ears. She had always wanted to know what white man had gotten Ruby pregnant with Jake.

Ruby said to Jake, "Ya'll gonna have to wait till this afternoon fo' I can tell ya that. Ya go on home now and wait till I come after ya."

He walked away, head hanging down, toward home.

As she put on her sweater and hat, Ruby looked at Sister Jesse and said, "Sister, will you finish washin' this heah dishes? I's got some business to take care of."

Jesse replied, "I'll be glad to." She was so curious she was about to burst, but she knew by the look on Ruby's face that she had better not ask any questions.

Ruby left the kitchen, walked out of the quarters, and disappeared down the road, looking very displeased. She walked and walked, finally coming to the front of the Stevens's plantation.

Mr. Stevens had been looking out the library windows and had watched Ruby come slowly up the long oak drive. He met her on the front veranda.

"Hey, Big Ruby gal!" he greeted her. "What brings you out here this time of day?"

Ruby bowed her hat-covered head and said, "I needs yo' help, sir," and she began to cry softly.

Mr. Stevens walked down the brick steps and put his arm around her broad shoulders. "Hush, now, don't cry. Things can't be all that bad. Let's us go into the library and talk," he said, trying to comfort poor distraught Ruby.

Entering the large, book-filled room, Mr. Stevens closed the double doors, seated Ruby in a velvet chair, and stood behind his oak desk.

Now Mr. Stevens had not been the same since Clara's murder and Bo's going into the service. Some said he had gone quite mad. Gazing sadly at Ruby, he asked, "What seems to be your problem, Ruby?"

Ruby started by saying, "Ya know, sir, I was jest a young gal when I worked over heah at the plantation for you and Miss Bootsy." She stopped, wiping her eyes with a hanky, and continued, "Well, I guess you has forgotten about the day we . . ." She looked around and in a low whisper said, "The day we made love out in the washhouse."

Nervously, Mr. Stevens cleared his throat and said, "No, I haven't forgotten that day, Ruby. Go on."

"Well, the truth is I fell fo' ya, sir. And that's why I left the plantation without so much as a word to you or Miss Bootsy. I knew we's could get into lots of trouble if anyone found out that I was with child," Ruby continued.

Mr. Stevens had to sit down.

"Later, I had a boy chile and that be Jake. Now Jake needs a last name so he can go join the army and I's don't know what to tell him his last name be," Ruby said, at last getting to the real reason for her visit.

Mr. Stevens sat there for what seemed a long time, staring off into space. Finally, he poured two small crystal glasses of sherry from a bottle on the desk. He handed one to Big Ruby and took one for himself.

"A toast to the boy, one of my boys," he said, raising his glass. They both drank.

"I guess you'll have to give him my last name," he said.

Ruby's face lit up. As tears sparkled in her eyes, she whispered, "Jake Stevens."

★ ★ ★

It was a bitterly cold day when the moving truck came to move all of our belongings to our new home. The coldness made things much harder to bear. It took the movers most of the morning to pack and load everything into the large truck. When they were finished, the driver turned to Mamma and said, "We're all packed, ma'am, and ready to go."

Mamma literally had to pull me from Big Ruby's arms. Tears streamed down my face as I bawled my heart out. How could I ever leave the safety and the love I felt in Ruby's warm arms!

Daddy waited in the packed car as Mamma pried me from Ruby and placed me in the back seat near the window. By now, Ruby was hunched over with shoulders shaking in grief. John, my dearest friend, broke away from his mother and ran to the window where I was. I rolled down the window and reached for his black hand, clasping it in mine.

John sobbed, "I's sho' gonna miss ya, Cotton Candy. Youse think we'll ever git to play together agin?"

I fell over on the crowded back seat and cried as if my heart were splitting in two. Everyone cried uncontrollably as we pulled out of the gravel drive from the Big House, leaving Dixie Roads forever.

Just as we turned the curve, I crawled up on my knees and looked out the back window with tear-filled eyes. I saw Big Ruby, John, Sister Jesse, Jewel, Amos, and Jake. I saw Doctor Theophrastus, Nell, Linda Gayle, Tom Edward, and Miss Neta holding Girthalene. For a split second, I thought I saw Clara waving to me out of the shadows. I could hear her beautiful soothing voice saying to me, "Hey, honey, you are a sugar cube. You and me is gonna get along just fine."

A couple of hours later, following closely behind the moving truck, we finally reached the gate of the army ammo plant. Still in a state of shock and half-asleep, I sat up to view my new surroundings. There was a big iron gate in front of the moving truck and a small guardhouse. A soldier had come out of the guardhouse and was talking to the truck driver. The gates swung open, and the guard waved for us to pass through. When we reached the guard, he put his gloved hand up for us to stop the car. He bent down, looking inside the car.

"Welcome to the Louisiana Ordinance Plant. I have told the truck driver how to get to your house. You will be in staff house

5," he said, saluting and motioning the car through the heavily guarded gates.

We proceeded past white office buildings much larger than the Big House. The main building looked like a picture of the White House I had seen on a calendar in Miss Neta's kitchen. I thought to myself, "Could it be that all this time Washington, D.C. was only a couple of hours from Dixie Roads?" For the first time that dreadful day, I got excited. I looked across the grounds to see if I might catch a glimpse of President Roosevelt. We pulled around a wide circle of pretty one-storied houses with well-manicured yards, then came to a stop in front of staff house 5.

We spent the rest of that day trying to get everything in its proper place. Mamma found the 1940s California-style ranch house to be very spacious. She loved it right away. She said it looked like a house she had seen in an issue of *Life* magazine. Later that night, after the movers had gone, Daddy built a fire in the fireplace in the new living room. We toasted marshmallows on coat hangers while Mamma made some hot chocolate in her modern kitchen all by herself without the help of Big Ruby and Sister Jesse.

The Christmas of 1945 we spent very quietly in our new home at the ammunition plant. Oh, there were lots of store-bought presents, a huge Christmas tree with electric lights, and a stocking hanging over the roaring fireplace, brimming over with candy, fruit, nuts, and firecrackers. But there was just something missing. After we opened our many gifts, we sat gazing into the fire, remembering last Christmas when Santa almost didn't show up in Dixie Roads . . .

★   ★   ★

John and I were busy playing tiddlywinks in the hall just off the kitchen. Our attention left the game when we heard Mamma tearfully saying to Big Ruby, "Oh, Big Ruby, I don't know what we are gonna do about Santa Claus this year. We just don't have any money. The cafes haven't made a cent in I don't know how long. Nobody has any money it seems. I guess it's cause of this ugly ole war. I guess Santa just isn't gonna show up this year."

By now, both women were sitting at the kitchen table, crying buckets into their coffee cups. Big Ruby finally dried her eyes on her apron and said to Mamma, "We must look a sight. Now, now, sugar. Dry yo' eyes, Miss Elsie. We's colored folks ain't never had no money at Christmas time and we's always had us a good time. You and Mr. William, don't ya'll worry none. Jest leave old Santa to Big Ruby. I'll get that scamp down the chimney somehows."

Mamma got up from the table and hugged Big Ruby. She said, "We just can't let this ole hateful war ruin our Christmas. I know if anyone can save Christmas for us, you can, Ruby gal."

Mamma left on her way down to the cafe. Ruby began clearing the table when she heard John and me in the hall.

She hollered, "John, Cotton Candy, ya'll come see me a minute."

We left the tiddlywinks on the floor and went into the kitchen. Big Ruby looked down on us with hands on her wide hips and said, "Were ya'll in there spyin' and listenin' to me and Miss Elsie?"

We shook our heads saying, "No, ma'am!"

Ruby said, "Well, never ya mind. Ya'll go on outside and play — and don't ya'll get nasty, neither. And ya'll stay out there until I call ya'll, ya heah? I's got a lot of thinking to do 'sides all my chores. Now git!"

John and I went out the back door. Crawling through the hedge to Miss Nell's, John said, "Cotton, I guess ya heard what yo' Mamma said. I guess Santa must be sick or something. What do ya think, Cotton?"

I thought for a minute, then replied, "I guess he's jest flat broke like everybody else. And he jest don't have time to fool with us down heah in Dixie Roads. Or maybe he's fighting the war overseas." I had visions of Santa in his reindeer-drawn sleigh flying over some faraway city, dropping bombs on our enemies.

With John and me out of her hair, Big Ruby called Sister Jesse, Jake, Jewel, and Amos together in the kitchen and told them what Miss Elsie had said about not being able to afford Christmas this year.

"Now ya'll know none of us has ever had much money at Christmas time, so we needs to put our heads together and show these white folks how us colored folks has a fine Christmas without no money! Now ya'll know what to do, so git to work," Ruby ordered.

The week before Christmas, the household became very secretive, with everyone disappearing most of the time. John and I got very bored with no one to talk to or play with. We were constantly being told not to come in, or to go away, or don't look in there, or plainly to just get lost! Everyone was acting strangely, that's for sure.

One cold sunny afternoon, Jake and Amos came by the busy kitchen to ask if John and I could go out into the woods with them to find a Christmas tree. Ruby said we could. John and I followed Jake and Amos out of the yard across a flat, dry cotton patch into the cold dense woods on the other side of Low Bayou. Jake carried an axe and Amos had a handful of tow sacks.

We all followed Amos into the sun-filtered frosty woods where he stopped in front of a large cedar tree and laid down the tow sacks.

"Dis one heah has a nice shape to it. What do ya'll think?" Amos remarked. We all agreed on the tree and Jake began cutting the cedar down.

Once it was on the ground, Amos said, "We'll leave the tree heah and pick it up on our way home. Now come on. We's got lots more things to gather in dis heah woods. Sister Jesse and Big Ruby wants some pinecones, holly berries, and mistletoe, and some privet hedge berries for decorations."

Jake gave John and me each a tow sack and told us to gather all the pinecones we could find. We picked the prickly pinecones off the ground while Amos climbed a big oak tree and threw down clumps of mistletoe with sticky white berries. We gathered dark green branches of holly with clusters of ruby-red berries and switches of privet hedge loaded with tiny purple berries. With sacks full, we started home, taking turns dragging the cedar tree.

On our way, we stopped at a big magnolia to gather some branches of the shiny leaves and seedpods.

Quietly, John asked me, "What we gonna do with all dis heah woods stuff?"

Sharp-eared, Amos said, "We's gonna make everythin' real pretty for ya'll's Christmas time. Jest ya wait and see."

We passed along the banks of Low Bayou, and Amos pulled handfuls of Spanish moss out of the trees. He put it in the sack with all the other treasures from the woods.

We entered the yard, loaded down. The womenfolk ran out of the kitchen, relieving us of the heavy sacks. Ruby looked at everything we had gathered, then said, "Ya'll go on in the house and get some hot coffee off the stove and some sweet tater pie. It was jest baked. Ya'll look like ya'll are half-frozen."

We mounted the sweet-smelling cedar on a stand and placed it in the living room near the front windows to be decorated later. Mamma and Daddy returned from the cafe, bringing with them some Christmas paint for Big Ruby. The whole backyard was transformed into a beehive of activity. Mamma and Ruby sprayed the privet berries silver and the magnolia leaves gold to make a centerpiece for the dining room table. The holly berries were arranged with candles in the middle on the mantel above the open fireplace. Daddy went into the attic and brought down all the decorations from Christmases past. Before long, the big house looked like Christmas Fairyland. It smelled of cedar and the cool fragrance of the woods

After supper, Jewel popped a huge bowl of popcorn, and we sat around the roaring fire and strung it for the tree. The big RCA radio played Christmas carols. We all joined in on "Silent Night" and "Jingle Bells." The tree was then completely covered with the spanish moss from Low Bayou. Ruby sprinkled the moss with Ivory Soap snowflakes. When she finished, the cedar tree looked as if it had been in a blizzard. We children wrapped the strings of popcorn around and around the tree. Candles were placed on every branch.

Ruby stood back, admiring the tree. She said, "Now, we won't light the candles till Christmas Eve. Oh, I almost forgot the finishin' touch."

She reached down into a cardboard box and brought the little angel that my grandmother had made years ago for the top of the tree. She said, "This looks jest like my little Cotton Candy!" as she handed the angel to Mamma.

Mamma and Daddy picked me up and told me to reach way up top and fasten the angel to the highest branch. Once the angel was in place, we all agreed that it was the prettiest Christmas tree in the civilized world. I was put in my warm bed that night with my heart brimming over with love.

Sister Jesse had a big secret that was just about to drive her crazy. She had been working on quilt covers for almost a year as gifts for Big Ruby and my family. She always worked on them in her private moments so nobody would see them. The one for Big Ruby was made from men's silk neckties. It was a rainbow of shiny colors. The one for Mamma had ladies with big bonnets on it and just lacked a few stitches. Sister Jesse would be so thankful to finish them and really proud to give them as Christmas presents.

Amos had gone into the pasture and found just the right chinaberry limb. He cut up some old innertubes and made slingshots for John, Jake, and me. As he worked on them he thought, "I hope these young'uns don't use this thing on me, ya know they is called nigger shooters." He laughed to himself as he whittled with his pocketknife.

Jake and Jewel had struck a bargain. If he would catch butterflies for her, she would dip them in paraffin and then Jake would mount them in little wooden frames that he had made with his pocketknife. They were beautiful pictures, and he had made one for each of us.

Jewel had made earrings and necklaces out of tiny seashells. Last summer, Miss Neta had gone to Galveston for her vacation and brought Jewel back a whole sack full of seashells that she had picked up on the beach. For the menfolk, Jewel had made tie clasps.

Ruby had been busy in the kitchen making fruitcakes for the whole neighborhood. Hers was the best fruitcake in the whole parish, according to Miss Neta. Her secret was bourbon whiskey, which she got from the Moonlite Cafe, but the most important ingredient was lots of love.

John and I had collected insects in mayonnaise jars. We had been busy catching all we could because that's what we were going to give everybody for Christmas.

Daddy had run into a man at the cafe who had been hurt in the war overseas and sent home. He had lots of souvenirs from the war for sale at a cheap price. Daddy had bought German army knives for all the men and Japanese silk scarves for all the ladies.

Mamma had talked the candy salesman from the cafe into selling her a whole box of bubble gum. Bubble gum was something, now, and none of us had ever seen any. She knew it would be a great treat! The salesman told Mamma that with the rationing of sugar bubble gum was as scarce as hen's teeth. She figured that everyone would get ten pieces and we would have to save it after we chewed it a while because it was so expensive.

Christmas Eve, Big Ruby dressed John and me in warm clothes, and we went round to all the neighbors and sang carols while Ruby handed out her delicious fruitcakes. When we got back home, Sister Jesse gave us hot spiced tea.

"It won't be long now before Santa Claus comes. Ya'll better go on up to bed and go to sleep so youse can get up and see what he brought ya," she said.

Everyone went to bed, but I know that no one slept a wink. It was truly a Christmas that none of us would ever forget. It was the Christmas when Santa almost didn't show up, but Big Ruby did . . .

★ ★ ★

Mamma broke our silence saying, "Big Ruby sure did make a good Santa. If it hadn't been for her, we would have had a pretty miserable Christmas last year."

Daddy said, "Ya'll remember how funny it was when Ruby was trying to show Sister Jesse how to blow a bubble with the bubble gum? And Jesse finally learned how to blow one and couldn't stop? The bubble got bigger and bigger until it popped all over her head and got all in her hair and made her eyes stick together."

John and I had chewed our gum until the pink gum turned gray. Then we let Linda Gayle and Tom chew it for a while until they got tired and then we took over.

We laughed and told stories about the Christmas of 1944, and in so doing, we enjoyed the Christmas of 1945.

Daddy said, "Well, you see . . ." looking around the room at all the many gifts, " . . . money can't buy everything."

★   ★   ★

The next morning, Mamma awakened us before dawn and fed Daddy and me a huge breakfast. While we were eating, she said, "I'm so glad I don't have to work at the cafes any more. Now, I can spend more time with Cotton. When you get to work today, hon, you might inquire as to where Cotton will be going to school."

I cringed at the word "school." I had started the first grade in Dixie Roads, and I didn't like it.

Daddy said he would, kissed us both good-bye, and headed out the door to his first day on the new job.

I helped Mamma unpack most of the morning. Around eleven o'clock, I got bored. Noticing this, Mamma said, "Cotton, why don't you get some of your toys and go outside and play? I have a jillion things to do."

I went into my new room, reached in the back of the closet, and pulled out my costume box. Ruby had packed it for me with my Cotton Queen dress neatly folded inside. I put on the familiar dress with hoops, added the gloves, tied a maroon sash around my long blond hair, opened the parasol, and walked outside to a little pine thicket that grew in the new yard beside the house. I set up my play-like house in the thicket. I must have made a dozen trips in and out of the make-believe house to the new house, gathering more of my toys to make it more homey. I got my tea set and my many dolls to play with on my final trip. On my way back to my make-believe house, I ran into Mrs. Tinsley, the lady next door.

She said, "Hey, there, honey, is your mamma home? I didn't know the Matthewses had a little girl, too. All anyone told me was that they had a little boy by the name of William Gene."

I said, "Pardon me, Miss Tinsley, but I be Cotton. Cotton Candy!"

With an odd look on her face, she went into the house and I went back to my make-believe. I sang and danced out in the thicket, setting up my new house. Later that afternoon, a big army-green school bus pulled to a screeching halt in front of the house next door, disrupting my make-believe and bringing me back to reality.

Three small boys about my age and one taller, older boy came spilling off the bus, roughhousing. They came running past the pine thicket where I was playing and when they saw me, they came to a dead stop, bumping into one another. They stood in front of me, mouths gaping.

Finally, Tommy Brandon, the oldest boy, who was about twelve, asked, "Who in the heck is that?"

Peter Brandon, Tommy's younger brother, said, "*What* is that?"

Billy Bob Long, brother to the other boy, Jerry, said, "I thought ya'll said a boy was moving into staff house 5."

Jerry Long said, "That's what my mamma told us."

They all turned as if they had seen a ghost and ran away.

I went into the house, walked directly to my room, and closed the door. I took off the hoops, dress, and other parts of the Cotton Queen costume and went into the kitchen where Mamma was busily working.

"Mamma, will you cut my hair?" I asked very seriously.

"Cotton, what has got into you?" Mamma asked. "Are you sure that's what you want?" I had never had my hair cut before.

"Yes, ma'am," I answered in a small voice.

She got her scissors, whispering a little prayer of thanks, and cut off my long blond hair. She tied the hair with a maroon ribbon and placed it in the family Bible.

"Now that you have decided to make a change, maybe we can call you by the name we gave you, William Gene," Mamma said.

I returned to my room and took a long look at the new little boy staring back at me in the mirror. I placed the costume and the past in the big box and whispered, "William Gene Matthews." I put the box in the back of the closet, where it remained, never to be brought out again.

Later, I went outside where the little boys were playing strange new games and asked if I could join in. From that day forward, I practiced very hard to become one of the "good ole boys."

Epilogue

Many years have passed and times have greatly changed since those warm, scented days I spent as a child in North Louisiana. The railroads are no longer of great importance, as they were in the forties, but every now and then I do run across an old train track. And, I am happy to say, the honeysuckle is still growing in wild abundance over the creosote-soaked crossties. The heady mixture always overwhelms me, and out of the imaginary train-smoke, I can hear Big Ruby calling the Cotton Queen to come and play!